Priscilla
the
Great

TO Emma, I hope you enjoy.

Sybil Nelson

Sybil Nelson

ISBN: 1453776273
ISBN-13: 9781453776278
Library of Congress Control Number: 2010912458

Chapter 1

Captured

I awoke tied to a chair. My eyes felt glued shut. I struggled to pry my eyelids apart. Once open, I shut them again as quickly as possible. A ridiculously bright and obnoxious light glared in my eyes, totally super-sizing my already painful headache.

"Holy hot dogs!" I said, borrowing my best friend's catch phrase.

"Good morning, Priscilla. Welcome back," an eerie voice said from … from everywhere. The deep, sinister voice surrounded me as if it poured out of the walls. I recognized that voice. I knew that man was evil!

"*Good* morning? I don't see what's so good about it. My head is killing me and that light you're shining in my face makes me want to dig my eyes out with a spoon!" I yelled into space.

"Sorry about that, Priscilla. We were trying to revive you. You've been out for a number of hours." The light faded away, allowing me to open my eyes fully without performing spoon surgery. There wasn't much to see. I sat in a stainless steel chair in the center of an otherwise empty stainless steel room.

The walls were smooth and cold-looking. Even the chair felt cold. I shifted in my seat, trying to warm up my butt cheeks.

"What do you want from me?" I asked, trying to hide the desperation in my voice. I mean, I was really scared. I'd been kidnapped. Really kidnapped. I wondered if they'd done that Amber Alert thing for me.

"You'll find out soon enough."

And then silence.

A few minutes later, a huge dude with an even huger gun walked into the room from a door I hadn't even noticed was there. It was almost like he'd melted through the wall.

He wore black pants and what looked like a sleeveless black bullet proof vest over a muscular chest. He easily could have been my dad's twin. He even had the exact same tattoo as my dad on his left arm, a big circle with a whole bunch of overlapping circles inside of it. It was too much of a coincidence. I knew my dad had been here before. I could feel it.

"How do you know she's the right girl?" a voice said in my head a little while later. No, wait, it wasn't inside my head. It was from somewhere else. And since Mr. Bodyguard didn't look like the talkative type, I knew it wasn't him speaking.

"Look at her. It has to be her. There's no way that resemblance is a mistake."

"But she obviously doesn't have any powers. If she did, she would have been out of that chair a long time ago."

The voices were coming from another room. My super hearing had returned, which meant my other powers would be back soon as well.

After a moment of silence, one of them said something that almost made my heart stop.

3

"Either way, she has to die."

Die? Oh my God, this was serious. Before I could panic, the calmness took over. I felt my powers surging. I started to formulate a plan.

Chapter 2

The Most Awful Thing
in the World

Wait. Let me back up, introduce myself, and explain how all of this started. My name is Priscilla Maxine Sumner, and I'm a good person. I used to be a good *normal* person, just a regular tomboy, until the Saturday before my seventh grade year. Then everything changed.

I remember that day so vividly, the day that changed my life, and honestly, I really didn't deserve it. Okay, so I did pour hot sauce into the twins' toothpaste. But *they* deserved it. They're the most awful five-year-old boys in existence. Trust me on that one. And I did tell my older brother's girlfriend that he liked to sing Christina Aguilera songs in the shower. Even though it's true, hunky football players apparently aren't supposed to sing girly pop songs. Who knew? And when my dad told me to clean my room before I could go to the pool party, I kinda just stuffed everything under my bed. But besides those tiny little things, I'm a really, really good person. No, I'm a great person. But really awful things always happen to me.

So I was standing next to the pool at Cali Crawford's house. She's the coolest girl in the seventh grade. The only way I even got an invite to the party was because her sister happens to be dating my Christina-Aguilera-singing brother.

Dad would only let me wear a one-piece to the party. How boring. He wouldn't even negotiate down to a tankini so I could show off a sliver of stomach. I mean, I'm already built like a stick figure. A bikini would have at least given me the illusion of curves. And you can't stuff a one-piece to create boobs. Believe me, I've tried. The tissue just fell down toward the stomach, making it look like I had cancerous alien tumors popping out of my gut.

Anyway, I was standing there, flat chest and all, when Spencer Callahan looked in my direction. Yes, he looked at me. I don't know why he would waste his effort and cast those perfect blue eyes on a scrawny redhead with no boobs in a boring one-piece, but he did. Not only did he look at me, but he actually stood up and walked toward me. So many thoughts flooded my mind, but the most prominent one was me as the future Mrs. Callahan. Mrs. Priscilla Callahan. We would have three children and two dogs. All girls. Even the dogs. After living with boys all my life, I couldn't take it anymore. Yeah, I had a mother, but she worked so much I sometimes forgot what she looked like.

"Hey, Priscilla. I wanted to ask you something." Oh my God. He was talking to me. And he wanted to ask me something. Did he want to ask me out on a date? It would be my first date. This was so exciting. I felt hot and flushed all over. I mean really, hot. So hot, in fact, even Spencer noticed.

"Do you—" He paused for a moment and his expression changed suddenly. "Are you okay?" he asked.

"Yeah, I'm fine. Why?"

"Well, you're all red. Are you sick?"

Oh my God. I was so ugly I looked sick.

He reached out and touched my forehead. "Priss, you're burning up," he said, yanking his hand away. "Maybe

7

you should go inside for a little while. Get out of the sun."

"I'm fine, really. I probably just ate some bad ... salsa."

"Salsa?" He squinted in confusion and then glanced at the snack table next to the barbeque grill. "There's no salsa here."

"Uh ... I bring my own. Love the stuff. Can't get enough of it. Take it everywhere I go."

"You take *bad* salsa with you everywhere you go?"

"Uh huh, yeah, everywhere. And right now, me and the salsa gotta go to the bathroom."

With that, I turned and tried to strut away as sexily (is that a word?) as possible, but it's pretty hard to look sexy when you feel like you're about to explode.

Once in the bathroom, I sat on the edge of the tub and placed my head in my hands. Though I felt hot all over, the heat was concentrated in my fingers. They were actually throbbing. I supposed I was radiating with embarrassment. *Did I really just say I had to go to the bathroom with some salsa?*

I filled the sink with water and splashed my face. I even stuck my whole head in the water. It didn't help.

I desperately needed to talk to Tai, my BFF. She would know what to do. She would whip out her iPhone and search the internet for answers, although I doubt she would find anything. This was without a doubt the weirdest thing ever. But it got worse.

I decided I needed to get out of Cali Crawford's house immediately and get to the safety of my own home. I reached for a hand towel to dry off, and as soon as I touched it, it burst into flames. Flames! I tossed it into the sink and watched as it sank beneath the water.

"Oh my God, oh my God, oh my God ..." That's when I heard a knock at the door.

"You okay in there, *Slum*ner?" It was Kyle Montgomery. It had to be. He was the only one that called me Slumner. He thought his little nickname was so clever. I thought it was lame. "Spence said you were sick. What'd you do, break a nail or something?"

"Go away, Kyle. I'm fine."

"I knew that. I knew you were fine. You're probably just so embarrassed about how bad I beat you in pool basketball."

"You only beat me by one point and that was because Spencer took his shirt off and totally distracted me." Besides Tai, Kyle was the only person on Earth who knew how I felt about Spencer. Even though Kyle was a complete jerk, I knew he'd never tell anyone. If he did, I'd tell everyone how he was so afraid of spiders that he called me over to his house at least once a week to kill one for him. Wimp.

"Whatever, Slumner. Just finish up whatever girly thing you're doing in there and get back out here for a rematch."

I rolled my eyes. He could be so maddening sometimes. He'd gotten even more obnoxious after he signed a modeling contract last summer. Sure he was cute in a kind of blond prep school boy kind of way, but his jerky personality totally canceled that out.

"Seriously, do you need me to get you some water or something? I don't want you getting heat stroke or anything."

"Just go back to the pool, Kyle. I'll be there to kick your butt in a second."

Amazingly, I didn't flip out any further at this point. That's huge for me. I always flip out. And considering I was trapped in a bathroom mysteriously setting things on fire, I think I have every right to panic. But I didn't. Instead, this calm feeling took over me. It was like someone had opened up my brain and poured smartness in. I needed ice and I needed it bad.

After a few seconds, I opened the bathroom door just a crack to make sure Kyle was gone. The door knob glowed red after I touched it. From the laughter and screaming outside, I could tell everyone was still by the pool. I opened the door a little farther, and after a quick survey, I high-tailed it through the hallway, past the family room, and then made a hard right toward the kitchen. Once there, I opened up the freezer and started shoveling ice down my suit. But that only gave me momentary relief from the heat. The ice melted as soon as it came in contact with my skin, making it look like I was standing in a puddle of my own pee.

I needed to do something before I became the first person in River's Bend history to spontaneously combust. Within seconds, the news would travel through town and then all of River's Bend, population 2,351, would be standing in Cali Crawford's house, shaking their heads at what was left of the crazy little Sumner girl. And they all thought I was crazy because I preferred riding my bike to painting my nails. And when I was little, instead of hosting tea parties like normal little girls, I handed out flyers inviting people to comic book conventions in my backyard. Unfortunately, the only people who ever came were my baby brothers, and that was because I bribed them with chocolate.

Suddenly, I spotted a fire extinguisher sitting on the counter next to the refrigerator. I grabbed it, pulled the pin, and sprayed myself. Ahh, sweet relief. Crisis averted. But then I heard footsteps coming down the stairs.

"What are you doing?" my older brother Josh asked, staring at the dripping mess.

"I ... I ... um ..." I didn't know exactly how to explain why I was standing in the Crawfords' kitchen covered in fire extinguisher foam. "Well, what are *you* doing?" I asked, turning the tables on him. "Yeah, what are you doing upstairs in the Crawfords' house without a shirt on?" That was partly a dumb question. I mean, Josh took his shirt off at every available opportunity so he could show off his six-pack abs. Once, at the grocery store, one of the twins spilled their juice box in front of this cute cashier who looked a little like Miley Cyrus. Well, since Josh thought he was as cute as a Jonas brother, he decided he needed to impress her. So, he whipped off his shirt and started cleaning up the mess. As if he ever cleaned up after the twins at home.

Josh started stuttering while turning different shades of red. He ran his fingers through his dark brown hair and shifted from foot to foot.

"Josh, what's taking so long? I'm thirsty," his girlfriend called from the top of the stairwell.

"Oooh, I'm telling Dad!"

"Shut up, freak," was his clever response.

"Freak? I'm not a freak. *I'm a genie in a bottle. You gotta rub me the right way.*" I started singing the Christina Aguilera song and gyrating in the kitchen, but I stopped abruptly when I almost slipped on the foam and water on the floor.

"That's it. We're leaving. If I don't get to have any fun, neither do you." Josh reached for a towel that sat on the kitchen counter. "Uh, Stef, I'll call you later. I gotta take my sister home," he yelled up the stairs. "You're the bane of my existence. Clean yourself up," he said to me, tossing the towel.

I flinched when it landed in my hands. I expected it burst into flames like the other one. But nothing happened. Absolutely nothing. *Did I just imagine the whole thing? Maybe it didn't happen. Or maybe it did happen and the episode just passed.* Neither scenario was comforting. I mean, if I imagined the whole thing that would mean I was some sort of crazy, hallucinating, psycho. But if I didn't imagine it, that would mean Josh was right. I *was* a freak.

Chapter 3
Hot Flashes

"Priscilla gorilla. Priscilla gorilla," the devil twins chanted while dancing around the living room in their matching blue jumpsuits. It was a stupid nickname since my skinny stature in no way resembled a gorilla. Even though it was pretty creative for five-year-olds, I really wasn't in the mood for their antics after the day I'd had.

I wish I knew how to conjure up the fire so I could singe their little blond heads. I thought for a second, but when nothing happened, I just stormed off to my room. I ditched the towel and bathing suit, put on some normal clothing—a Wonder Woman t-shirt and jean shorts— and then called Tai. She was off at space camp, or math camp, or science camp, or whatever hole in the Earth they send really smart twelve-year-olds to, to make them really smarter.

Tai was my absolute best friend since "The Era of Unfortunate Hair" a.k.a. third grade. My mother had just gone back to work full-time so it was my dad's first attempt at the stay-at-home thing. He tried his best but just could not control my thick, unruly head of red hair. And apparently no one told him that there was an unwritten rule about the maximum number of scrunchies someone can wear at once. He had put so many in my hair that it was like they were growing out of my head. I looked like a multi-colored octopus. It was awful.

Anyway, in walked Taiana Houston. Her hair was just as pitiful as mine. She looked like she had gotten beaten in the head by a big lopsided ball of black tumbleweed. For some reason a single solitary braid protruded out of one side, and what looked like half of a beaded necklace dangled out of the other side. She was a black girl adopted by an old white couple who had no idea what to do with her kinky hair. We took one look at each other and fell on our butts pointing and laughing. And after two months of scouring hair magazines and experimenting with different things, we finally got our hair under control.

"How was the party?" she asked excitedly before even saying hello. She knew I had been looking forward to it for two weeks.

"Awful, just awful," I said, holding back tears. I flopped on my bed and twisted the phone cord around my fingers. As if it wasn't bad enough that I wasn't allowed to have a cell phone, I was forced to use one of those ancient home phones with the long curly cord attached to it.

"I'm sure it wasn't that bad, Priss. Just calm down and tell me about it."

After a brief recap of the day, Tai, my supposed best friend in the world, started laughing.

"Oh, you are the worst friend ever! Why are you laughing at me?"

"Oh my God. Bad Salsa? In all the practice Spencer conversations we've had, I never remember bringing up condiments." Tai continued to laugh. I imagined she was rolling around on the floor, clutching her stomach.

"You keep laughing at me and we are seriously going to have to rethink this friendship."

"I'm sorry, Priss," she said, trying to get control over herself. "Okay, I'm good. Just tell me, what in the world were you thinking?"

"I wasn't thinking. I was too afraid of spontaneous combustion. I mean, I think I've turned into the Human Torch!"

"The what?"

"The Human Torch. From the Fantastic Four. He can turn into fire."

"I'm sure you're exaggerating that part."

"No, I'm not, Tai! You had to be there. I set a towel on fire!"

"Well, I'm sure there's some physiological explanation. Your body heat probably rose from the embarrassment, causing a spike in your core temperature. And considering the fact that you've been in love with Spencer since the third grade, I'm sure your hormones were going crazy. And I bet you're close to your time of the month."

I turned my head and looked at the calendar on my wall. Snap. It was close to my time. Why did she always have to be right?

"I'm sure it felt like fire, but it was probably something a little less dramatic."

"I'm not exaggerating. Flames, I tell you. Flames!" I threw my hands in the air for emphasis as if she could see me. "Something strange is going on."

Tai was silent for a minute. I think I'd finally stumped my genius best friend. "Fire, huh? I'll look into it. But until I find something, why don't you ask your mom about it?"

"Sure. Right. Talk to my mom. I'll just grow some wings, fly to Brazil, and interrupt one of her drug deals." My mom worked for some big pharmaceutical company and traveled the world giving sales pitches. I usually just told people she was a drug dealer, though, because it sounded cooler and gave me some street cred. Well, in my head at least.

Why was Tai always trying to fix the unfixable relationship between my mother and me? Three years ago my mother didn't show up for my tenth birthday party. That's when I realized she thought her job was more important than her family. Since then we'd barely spoken. There was no way I was going to talk to that woman about something so personal and embarrassing. For now, I'd just consider my episode some sort of hot flash like women get in menopause. That would explain why it came and went. Flashes don't last forever. Kind of like the flash of hope I had that Spencer Callahan could possibly be interested in me. Flashes come and go and … oh, snap, one was coming.

"Tai, it's happening again!"

"Oh, oh, okay, uh … stand up and … and put the phone down and … and don't touch anything until it passes."

I jumped off the bed, dropped the phone, and stood with my hands and feet apart like I was about to get frisked by the police. It felt as though the heat started in my chest and radiated outward, landing in my hands. My fingertips pulsed, and there was smoke coming out of them! Just when I was about to scream because I was so freaking freaked out, a calm feeling came over me. I knew that if I just stayed still and didn't touch anything, the heat would pass and everything would be fine.

But, of course, my life couldn't be that simple. Just as my hands started turning an odd shade of red, there was a knock at the door, followed by, "Priss, it's Dad."

Chapter 4
Dubai, Brazil

"Priss, are you okay in there?" Dad asked when I didn't respond immediately.

"Um, uh …" I stuttered, not thinking quickly enough to give a good answer.

Then he busted through the door like a cop in one of those Lifetime movies where the hero has to save the teenage daughter of his love interest from a coke-dealing pimp. I wasn't too surprised, though. It wasn't the first time he had knocked my door right off its hinges. Dad was always a little overprotective when it came to the safety of his children, especially me for some reason.

"What's wrong? What's going on?" His eyes were wild as he surveyed my room for some hidden danger.

"I'm fine, Daddy. I'm totally fine," I said, rolling my eyes.

My dad pushed his glasses farther up his nose and adjusted his tie. Yes, my stay-at-home dad wore a tie in the middle of a Saturday afternoon. At six foot five and nearly three hundred pounds of solid muscle, he looked too darn scary if he wore anything less formal. I mean, with his bald head and mysterious tattoos, the man was a spandex leotard away from looking like the next WWE champion.

"What are you doing?" he asked, resting his eyes on me for the first time and noting my awkward stance.

Deciding the only way out of this was a "Prissy Fit," as Josh so lovingly referred to them, I yelled, "Oh my God, Dad. You can't just bust into a girl's room unannounced! I'm a girl. I need privacy. What if I had been doing … girl stuff? You're so embarrassing. I want to die. Just die."

"Sorry, Priss. I thought you were in trouble," he said, turning around to pick my door up off the floor. He could be so paranoid sometimes. He wouldn't even let my school put my picture in the yearbook, saying he was afraid of child predators or something. "So, what kind of *girl stuff* do you call that move there?" he asked.

I looked up at my hands still reaching for the sky. My fingers had stopped pulsing and I felt the hot flash passing. Now I just had to figure out a way to answer Dad without making him totally spazz.

"Uh, it's a new dance move," I said, waving my hands in the air.

"Really?" he said, joining me in my made up dance to imaginary music.

I stopped moving and stared at him, holding in laughter. "You look ridiculous, Daddy." I mean, he really did look crazy. Imagine a body-building secret service agent trying to get jiggy. That about sums it up.

"*I* look ridiculous? You started it." He wrapped his arm around me and kissed the top of my head.

"What's going on? What happened?" Tai said over the phone. I looked around for the phone and noticed that it had slipped under the bed. But I heard her so clearly, like she was right next to me. How could that be?

"Did you hear that?" I asked my Dad, thinking maybe he had added some new technology to the antique piece of trash I called a phone.

"What?" he replied completely confused.

Hmph. Guess not. Maybe I had super hearing as well. Oh, that would be awesome. It would come in handy for those sneak attacks from the devil twins.

"Nothing, never mind." I sat down on the bed and crossed my legs Indian style.

"Are you sure you're okay? You look … different to me."

Oh, no. Could he tell I was somehow turning into a freak? Oh, how embarrassing.

"I guess you're just growing up," he said, shrugging off his concern. "We have a video chat with your mom in half an hour; then you can help me finish dinner. I'm making your favorite: spinach lasagna, broccoli casserole, and lemon meringue pie for dessert." My dad rubbed his hands together, excited over his homemade dinner.

"Okay, Dad."

"And don't be late. It's almost midnight in Dubai and your mom needs to get to sleep."

"Dubai? What part of Brazil is that?" I asked, thinking Dubai really didn't sound like a Portuguese word. But, hey, what did I know?

"Um, it's … it's, um, in the east part." He looked uneasy. His blue eyes darted back and forth around the room. Was he hiding something from me?

My dad picked up the door, stepped through the gaping hole, and then leaned it against the doorframe to give me as much privacy as possible. I knew he'd probably reattach it after dinner. I wasn't too worried about it. What I was worried about was the Dubai-Brazil thing. I mean, I wasn't any kind of geography genius or anything, but I knew that Brazil was in South America. There was no way any part of Brazil could be like nine hours ahead of Pennsylvania. It didn't make any sense. An image of a map popped in my brain. It was the map on the wall of my sixth grade teacher's classroom. Why could I suddenly see every detail of it in my mind? There was no Dubai in Brazil. In fact, according to my suddenly perfect memory, Dubai was in the Middle East. Right smack dab in the middle of the Middle East. My heart sank. What was he hiding from me?

Suddenly, I remembered Tai was still on the phone.

"You there, Tai?" I asked after grabbing the phone and resting it between my ear and shoulder. I needed my hands free so I could dig out the globe stuffed under my bed. Maybe I was remembering wrong. I had to be sure. I had to know.

"Priss, Dubai is nowhere near Brazil," she said immediately. She'd heard the entire conversation. "Your dad lied to you," she added.

"Yeah, I know."

Chapter 5

A Deal's a Deal

I thought about confronting my dad about the whole Brazil-Dubai thing, but Mom totally covered for him during the video chat. She said she was in Brazil yesterday and had just flown to Dubai that morning. That explained it, right? Wrong. Dad didn't say she went to Brazil and then Dubai. He specifically said Dubai was in Brazil. There was definitely something else going on.

Every Saturday afternoon we all gathered around the computer screen and talked with my long-distance mother so we could pretend like we were a family. I thought about taking Tai's advice and asking her about hot flashes, but how could I do that in front of my three brothers and my dad? It just wasn't going to happen. Besides, the Saturday chats never turned into anything productive. We usually just ended up fighting. It was annoying to have to interrupt my day for a woman who couldn't care less about me.

"So, what's going on in your life, Priscilla?" my mother asked after talking to Josh about football practice and to the twins about their new dolls—I mean, action figures.

"What do you care?"

"Priscilla, you watch your tone," my dad barked.

"It's okay, Greg. She just asked a question." My mother took a deep breath and gathered her long red hair into a tight ponytail. "Despite what you might think, I really do care about what goes on in your life. Now, didn't you have a pool party today? Why don't you tell me how it went?"

"If you really care about what goes on in my life, how about being around more often than the seasons change? Why can't you be a normal mother and go to PTA meetings and back-to-school shopping with your children?" My mother pushed her glasses farther up her nose. Nothing ever flustered her, not even my scathing sarcasm. Just once I'd love to see some emotion from her. But, no, she never lost her cool. Everyone left that to Dad.

"That's it, Priss. I've had enough of you," my father yelled. "Apologize right now then go to your room!"

"Sorry ... Mother." I hoped she put those two words together and got the true meaning of that sentence.

The next morning I woke up with a headache the size of Josh's ego. My eyes hurt, my ears hurt, and my whole body tingled. It kinda felt like sharp little bugs were crawling around in my body and trying to escape through my skin. I decided I needed to soak in a hot bath.

When I got to the bathroom, Josh was just stepping out surrounded by swirling steam like he was coming out of a sauna or something. I bet he'd used up all the hot water ... again. He was such a prima donna, spending literally hours in the bathroom every day.

"Stupid meat head!" I yelled after I felt the frigid water. I let it run for a while and it wasn't getting any warmer. Then I had an idea. I might as well put this fire thing to good use. I filled the tub, then tried to think hot thoughts. Nothing. *Okay, what did I do the other two times it happened? Nothing. It just happened.* Then I remembered something. Both times I had the hot flashes, I was thinking about Spencer Callahan and how much ... *whoa, that brought the heat.* I stuck my hands in the water just long enough to get it nice and toasty.

This might not be so bad after all. But if I was going to use this fire thing to my advantage, I really had to learn how to control it. I had to figure out a way to bring the heat without thinking about Spencer.

* * *

After spending the morning perfecting my fire-shooting technique, I headed to McMillan's pharmacy. With my time of the month approaching, I really needed to buy some "supplies," but after peeking through the window and seeing Trevor Callahan working the register, there was no way I was going in. I was not about to let the brother of my dream boy catch me buying those God-awful things.

I was just about to give up and go home when I saw Kyle ride by on his bike.

"Hey, Kyle, you up for a challenge?" I called out to him.

"What'd you have in mind?" He turned and rode up to the store front.

"Race to town square gazebo and back."

"Bikes or feet?"

I looked him up and down. As usual, Kyle was dressed a little too nicely for a lazy Sunday afternoon in River's Bend. He always wore these fancy Italian shirts that probably cost way too much money, along with pleated pants. He looked good, but like I said before, too preppy for my taste. He even had a pair of shiny brown loafers on. Loafers. Who wears loafers to ride their bike? That's when I made my decision.

"Feet." He'd never be able to keep up with me in those shoes.

"What are the stakes?" he asked.

"If you win, I'll give you back that Spider-Man comic you lost to me last week."

Kyle smoothed a wrinkle out of his shirt and pretended like he wasn't intrigued. That was his favorite comic and I knew he wanted it back.

"If I win, I get the comic and you get poop duty for a month."

"You mean you're not potty trained yet, Kyle?" I said with a smirk.

He glared at me. "You know what I mean."

I knew what he meant. I just like messing with him. He meant poop duty for our dog, Max Montgomery. Max was a cute little chocolate lab that we found by the river when we were little. We took him home and named him Max after my middle name, Maxine, and Montgomery after Kyle's last name. Then we took turns taking care of him until one day Max got tired of being tormented by the twins and stayed at Kyle's house permanently. So I just went over every day to help.

"Fine, but if I win, you have to buy me something from McMillan's."

"Is that all? Deal, Slumner. You're on."

Two minutes and forty three seconds later, I had him beat.

"You're pretty fast ... for a girl," he panted with his hands on his knees. He always had to add that "for a girl" part whenever I beat him. It made me so mad.

"Whatever, Kyle. I beat you fair and square."

"Fine," he said, standing up straight. "What do I have to buy for you?" He ran his fingers through his blond hair, which still looked perfectly styled even after running three blocks and back. How did he do that?

I stood on my tip-toes and whispered in his ear.

"Oh no, no, no. God, no. No way, Slumner."

"You have to. I beat you. A deal's a deal."

"Fine," he said, snatching the ten dollar bill out of my hands and storming into the store.

I watched through the window as Kyle made his way to the *female* aisle. I could tell by the shade of crimson that crept over his face that he'd never been there before.

Why the heck are there so many choices? a voice in my head said. Wait a minute. It wasn't in my head. It was Kyle. I could hear him from inside the store. He whispered to himself as he turned around in circles. I think he was sweating more than when we were running through town. *Long, thin, regular, super, dry weave, and wings. Wings? Who needs wings? Is she buying a maxi pad or a magic fairy that lives in her pants?*

I had to cover my mouth to hold in a giggle. I should make Kyle buy these things for me all the time. It was much more entertaining.

"Thinking about buying some more bad salsa?" a voice said from behind. I spun around and stared into the beautiful baby blue eyes of Spencer Callahan.

A rush of heat filled me as I saw his perfect, pink, plump lips curve into a smile. He had apparently just skateboarded down Main Street so he was a little out of breath, so instead of breathing he was more like panting, and every time he exhaled, my bangs blew off of my forehead. That's how close he was standing to me. I could smell his Mentos-scented breath, and it made me weak.

I thought I would faint, but then a hot flash woke me up. *Oh snap! What would I do now?* An image of a snake popped in my head, a poisonous snake. If a snake bit itself, would it die? No. It would be immune to its own venom. With that thought in mind, I clasped my hands together like I was about to sing "Mary Had Little Lamb" at a kindergarten recital. It stung a little, but I didn't burst into flames. And I hoped Spencer didn't notice the thin stream of smoke rising from my hands.

"Bad salsa?" I asked, trying to figure out what the heck he was talking about. Then it hit me. That was my stupid response at the pool party. "Oh, I don't know. I'm thinking about expanding my condiment options. I'm looking into bad ketchup, bad mustard, and bad guacamole."

Spencer chuckled. "That was funny. That was really funny, Priss." He stared at me as if he was shocked that I could say something funny. Actually, I was shocked, too. "Anyway, what I wanted to ask you—"

Just then, Kyle burst through the door and shoved a package into my chest.

"I hate you, by the way," he muttered before doing that little shiver people do when they think something is really gross. He hopped on his bike and said, "I think I need a shower," before speeding off.

"What was that about?" Spencer said, looking from me to where Kyle was riding off. Thankfully, my supplies were wrapped up in a brown paper bag so he couldn't tell what they were.

I shrugged. "Just Kyle being cranky, I guess. I think the peroxide from all that hair dye is seeping into his head."

Spencer laughed at that, but I actually felt kinda bad that I'd said something so mean about Kyle. He was a jerk most of the time, but I still considered him a friend. Kind of.

"Anyway," he said, "I'm having a few friends over tomorrow night. Kinda to celebrate our last night of freedom before school starts. Why don't you come?"

Did he just ask me to his house? That's like a date kinda, right? I was going on a date with Spencer Callahan! I was too shocked to say anything so I just nodded.

"Sweet. We're gonna start at like five after my dad finishes his Labor Day party stuff. We'll just watch some movies or something." He picked up his skateboard then pushed the door of the pharmacy open. "Is Tai back in town yet?" he asked before entering.

"Her flight gets in tomorrow morning," I said, surprised that my lips still worked. I couldn't believe I was going on a date with Spencer Callahan.

"Sweet. She can come, too."

Oh my God. I was seriously going to faint. How nice of him to invite my best friend too!

I plopped the package into the Batgirl basket at the front of my bike and prepared to hustle back home. I told my dad I was only going to get an ice cream at Willie's Sweet Shop so I literally had about two minutes and thirteen seconds before he sent Josh looking for me or, worse, he came for me himself. The last time that happened, he ended up busting into the library with tears in his eyes, sweeping me up into a bear hug and totally pulling me away from a classic Ms. Marvel comic. He said that when I didn't come home on time, he got worried. Hmph. Now that I thought about it, he really did worry about me a lot.

My dad really loved me. And despite his scary pro-wrestler appearance, he was extremely smart. I mean like Tai smart. He had degrees in biochemistry and engineering. Though nowadays the only time he had to use either was when the twins put a peanut butter sandwich in the DVD player. Dad took it apart, cleaned it, and then rewired it himself. He was a genius. Now if only he could figure out a way to rewire the twins into something less gross and annoying.

Chapter 6

Monster Alien

When I got home, Josh was sitting at the kitchen table, looking totally depressed. I resisted the urge to turn on a Christina Aguilera song just to bug him and decided to actually talk to him.

"What's up, Josh?" I grabbed a bottle of Gatorade out of the refrigerator and sat across from him.

"Nothing. Leave me alone," he said. He had been spinning a small gold ring on the table, but when I sat down, he tossed it into a little black box and then stuffed it into his pocket.

"What's that?" I asked.

"Nothing." He crossed his arms and leaned back in the wooden chair. "I don't want to talk about it," he said. I knew he was lying. If he really didn't want to talk about it, he would've gotten up, called me a nosey brat or something worse, and then gone to his room. But he didn't. He just sat there, which meant he really wanted to talk but didn't want to make the first move.

"What's that in your pocket?" I asked, finishing off the Gatorade. I didn't realize how thirsty I was. I wondered if that had something to do with the fire.

Josh rocked back in the chair and didn't answer. I could tell he was trying to decide whether he should tell me some secret or not. "You wouldn't understand. You're just a kid."

"I'm not a kid. I'm a woman. In fact, I have a date tomorrow." I lifted my chin in the air like royalty and looked down my nose at him.

He rolled his eyes. "A date? You're only twelve. You don't know anything about dating. Does Dad know about this?"

My eyes expanded. Dad would absolutely not allow it. I didn't even think about that when I agreed to go to Spencer's house. "Oh my God, Josh. Don't tell him, please. He won't let me go. He'll flip out. Please, Josh, this is my one chance at happiness. Please don't ruin it for me, please!"

Josh got an evil smirk on his face. He would definitely tell Dad and enjoy doing it. I thought my life was over. But then his expression changed. His blue eyes softened and he bit his bottom lip like he was thinking about something. Then he leaned forward in the chair and said, "I'll keep your secret if you keep mine."

What? Josh was actually going to confide in me? This was new. After nodding my acceptance of the deal, he reached into his pocket and pulled out the little black box. He opened it up and revealed a skinny little gold ring.

"What's that?" I asked slightly confused. What was so important about a thin, cheap-looking ring?

"I'm going to give it to Stefanie."

"Why?"

"Because I love her and I want to spend the rest of my life with her."

"You're going to propose?" I was glad I'd finished the Gatorade because if I'd still been drinking I would have spit it across the table.

"Not exactly. It's a promise ring. It means that I promise to propose to her one day."

"So … that means you're like engaged to be engaged."

"Yeah, I guess so."

I wanted to tell him that was like the stupidest thing I'd ever heard. He was only sixteen. There was no way he could know who he wanted to spend his life with at sixteen. I mean, eight months ago he probably would've married that cartoon warrior with the big boobs on his favorite fighting game. And now he suddenly wanted to marry his first real girlfriend. But then again, who was I to talk? I knew I would be marrying Spencer Callahan. And I was even younger than Josh.

But why did it have to be Stefanie Crawford? There was something about that girl I just didn't like. It could've been the fact that she had the annoying habit of stretching her chewing gum into a long strand out of her mouth and then wrapping it around her finger before plopping it back in. Or it could've been that she had bleached her dark hair so many times that it looked like long strands of straw. I had gotten over the fact that after dating my brother for six months, she still called me Patricia, but what bothered me the most was the way she ordered my brother around. I would think a big football player like Josh would stand up to her and tell her to hold her own purse when she went to the bathroom, but he was so completely in love with her that he did just about anything she said.

"So if you're so in love with her, why did you look so depressed when I walked in?"

He shrugged. "What if she doesn't feel the same way? What if she rejects me?"

"I don't even think that's possible. I mean, besides the Christina Aguilera thing, you're a pretty good catch."

In fact, he was way too good for Stefanie Crawford. I wanted to give him my opinion of Stefanie, but when I saw the way he stared at the ugly ring with that lovesick puppy look, I knew it wouldn't have mattered. So, I just said congratulations and went to call Tai.

"Bad news, Priss," Tai said, once again before I even said hello. "I couldn't find any medical reason for why you'd be able to shoot fire."

"Forget that, we have more important things to discuss," I said, kicking off my sneakers and hopping on top of my bed.

"What can be more important than fire shooting out of your fingers?"

"How about what I'm going to wear on my date with Spencer Callahan?"

Tai screamed so loudly I had to pull the phone away from my ear. Of course, I wanted to scream as well, but I didn't want my dad knocking the door down again.

Tai and I spent so much time making plans for Spencer's party that my dad practically had to drag me out of my room for dinner. By the time I got to the table, everyone was already eating and my plate of pork chops was cold. But after spending all morning practicing, I was slowly becoming an expert at bringing the hot flashes. I figured out that it was kind of like accessing a part of my brain that had been locked. I could almost see myself turning a key inside my mind and opening up the hidden chamber that brought the heat.

So I decided to try it out on my dinner. After turning the key in my head, I felt the heat flow through my body and land in my fingers. I touched my plate of food and discreetly warmed up my pork chop, even turning it over once with my fork. Then I took a bite and smiled, truly impressed with myself and my new hidden talent.

I wondered when I would be confident enough to reveal it to my family. But then I thought maybe it would be more fun just to keep it to myself. What happened next kind of ruined that idea.

"Oh, Priss, it must be cold by now. Let me warm it up for you." My dad reached for my plate before I could stop him. As soon as he touched it, he yelped in pain then let the plate crash to the floor.

He stared at me with eyes filled with … terror. Was he afraid of me?

"What happened?" Josh asked, looking up. The twins barely noticed the disturbance and continued throwing broccoli at each other.

My dad went to the sink and placed his hand under running water. He didn't say anything.

"You okay, Dad?" Josh was starting to worry about my father's odd silence.

"I'm fine," he said finally while wrapping his hand in a towel. "I'm going to go to the basement for a while. Josh, can you clean up this mess. Priss, make sure the twins finish their food." He spoke as if someone had just died, and he wouldn't look me or Josh in the eye. Then he sulked off to the basement. I went to follow him, but the door was closed and locked by the time I got there.

The basement was absolutely off limits to all of us kids. After watching *The Wizard of Oz* when I was seven, I asked Dad if we could hide in the basement if there was a tornado, and he said we would be safer in the tornado than in the basement. I thought he was joking at first, but he didn't crack a smile. I never asked to go in the basement again.

I sat with my back against the door and waited for him to come out. Part of me wanted to talk to him and find out what was going on. He knew that plate shouldn't have been hot. Did he know I did it? But then again, maybe I didn't want to talk to him. Maybe the truth was too scary. And who says he would tell me the truth anyway. He'd already lied to me about the Dubai Brazil thing.

The way he looked at me made me want to cry. He must've thought I was some sort of monster or alien or monster alien. What if I *was* an alien? That would explain so much. Maybe that's why I didn't look like my dad or my brothers. I had this awful thick red hair and green eyes while Dad and Josh had dark hair and blue eyes. And the twins had blond hair and blue eyes. I shook my head. That couldn't be it. Unfortunately, I looked almost exactly like my mother. Wait a minute. What if my mother and I were the aliens? Maybe she wasn't in Dubai or Brazil, but on our home planet. Maybe my dad was in the basement making arrangements to send me back to my planet because I could no longer fit in with the human children.

My heartbeat raced. I had trouble breathing. I didn't want to live with monster aliens. A voice inside my head told me to calm down. Wait a minute. It didn't come from my head. It came from the basement. I could hear someone talking in the basement. I closed my eyes and concentrated on the voices.

"I can't calm down, Quin," my father said to my mother, probably through a video chat. "Something's happening to her." Oh my God. Were they talking about me?

"Well, if she is changing, we'll just have to deal with it," my mother said.

"This puts us all in danger. Maybe we should send her away. For her own safety."

"Gregory, please, don't panic. It's probably nothing. How many times did we think something was happening to Josh? It always turned out to be a mistake. Just watch her for a few days and let me know what you see. Then we'll decide what to do."

"I love you, Quin."

"I love you, too."

"Be safe."

"I will. I'll be home soon."

When I heard my father turn off the computer, I got up and ran to my room. After closing and locking the door, I paced the room and tried to calm my nerves. What did they mean, send me away? Where would they send me? I was beyond freaked out. I got out a sheet of Paper and a pen and tried to make a list like Tai does when she has a problem. But I could only think of two things to write: 1. What was happening to me was definitely not normal, and 2. I was somehow putting my whole family in danger.

Chapter 7

Waffle Attack

The next morning, I sat in my room minding my own business. Well, kinda minding my own business. I was staring at the Houston house with my binoculars, waiting for Tai to get home, but that's not really spying. She's my best friend and I hadn't seen her in three weeks and I needed to know as soon as she got in because we really needed to talk. I promised myself that I wouldn't use my fire power or super hearing again until I talked to her and we figured some things out. I also wanted to convince my parents I was normal so they wouldn't send me away.

In any case, I was completely the victim in an attack from the devil twins. They snuck into my room and nailed me in the head with two frozen waffles. Those little brats had great aim for five-year-olds. Then they ran out of the room laughing. I had to follow them and teach them a lesson. I had no choice. They can't just come into a girl's room unannounced and throw frozen waffles. They got one of my favorite comic books wet.

I caught up with Charlie first. I picked him up and threw him on the couch. Then I sat on him and farted. Yeah, I farted. So what? When dealing with little brothers, sometimes you have to get gross. Then I took his shoe laces and tied them around his wrists so that they were like attached to his feet. Unfortunately, Charlie thought this was hilarious, his idea of an awesome Monday morning. He was laughing the whole time. Even when I let him go and he had to hop around the house bent over with his butt sticking up in the air, he was still laughing. I rolled my eyes in disgust and went in search of Chester.

"Chessie, where are you?" I called sweetly. "I have some candy for you." He didn't fall for it. Those boys were getting smarter every day.

If I concentrated hard enough I could probably hear him giggling somewhere in the house. But I made a promise to myself that I wouldn't use my … oh, what the hay.

* * *

"Priscilla, what did you do to your brother?" my dad asked a few minutes later while I sat in the window seat of my room.

"You're gonna have to be more specific than that, Dad. I got too many of them."

"What did you do to Chester?" he said slowly, holding back his annoyance with me.

"Uh, well, let me just say, he totally deserved it."

"Priss, he's only five. I don't think anything he could do warrants you tying him to a chair and setting him on the street corner with a sign that says: Take me, I'm free."

"Sorry, Dad."

"Sorry's not good enough. Now I'll give you a choice. I can ground you for a week or you can make it up to them."

"Grounded?" I shrieked, turning to face him for the first time. "But, Dad, they started it!"

"And I'm finishing it."

I sighed. "Fine. I'll take them to the park after school tomorrow."

"Thank you," he said, but didn't leave the room. I looked out the window again and continued my stalking of the Houston house. "Is there anything you want to talk about, Priss?" he asked, sitting on my bed. I felt a little uneasy. For the first time in my life, I felt uncomfortable around my dad. I knew for a fact that he had lied to me. I didn't know if I could trust him anymore.

"Like what, Dad?" I didn't look at him. I just kept staring at Tai's house, willing her to come home.

"I don't know. What's going on in your life?" He took his glasses off and cleaned them with his tie.

He was trying to reach out to me, but I wasn't ready. I didn't know what to think of the conversation I'd overheard the night before. "Just watch her for a few days," my mother had said as if I was some sort of chemistry experiment.

I shrugged. "Nothing special." Well, that was the biggest lie ever told.

"Are you sure? Because a boy called here for you."

"Really? Who?" I asked, bolting upright. Was it Spencer? Did he really call me? How'd I miss that? Maybe he called while I was outside tying up Chessie. Maybe he wanted to confirm our date. More likely he suddenly realized what a loser I am and wanted to cancel.

"Kyle Montgomery," my father said.

I rolled my eyes and sat back down at my window seat. "Kyle is not a boy. He's ... he's just Kyle."

"Well if any young man intends on courting my daughter, he needs to first be properly introduced to me."

I laughed. "Daddy, you've known him since he was born. We have a picture of him poking your eye at my second birthday party."

Just then, I saw the Houston car pull up.

"Look, Daddy, if Kyle ever intends to ... court me or whatever, I'll definitely let you know, right after I puke." I didn't wait for a response. I dashed out of my bedroom and out of the house. I didn't stop running until I was down the street and in front of Tai's house. I hugged her so hard we both nearly fell over.

After the hugging and jumping up and down subsided, Tai grabbed my hand and pulled me inside her house. We pounded the shag carpeted stairs and then entered her bedroom. She locked the door, pulled the curtains shut, and then said, "Okay, show me."

"Show you what?" I said, acting confused.

"Oh, you know what. Show me the fire."

She pulled her thick black hair into a bun and slapped on a spare pair of glasses that were on her desk. Then she stared at me, banging her little fists together in anticipation. I hadn't seen her this excited over something since the high school science teacher let her visit the ninth grade biology class and dissect a pig.

"I don't know what you're talking about," I said, strolling around her bedroom and looking at her collection of books as if I'd never seen them before. Tai didn't have a normal twelve-year-old girl's bedroom. Neither did I, for that matter, but at least my room was fun. Half of my room was dedicated to Marvel comics and the other half to DC comics. Tai's room was just covered with books. And not cool books with pictures or anything. Just thick, boring, brown books with strange titles like *Quantum Mechanics* and *Vector Analysis*. And those were the books whose titles I could actually pronounce. Her room reminded me of a psychiatrist's office. Which I guess worked since I usually went over there to get help with my problems.

"Priscilla Maxine Sumner, if you don't show me right now I'll … I'll … I'll never speak to you again." She was so unimaginative with her threats. It would have been so much funnier if she threatened to dye my hair green or threatened to tell the twins that my comic book collection was a new type of toilet paper. But Tai wasn't very creative like that. But maybe that was why we were such good friends. We balanced each other out.

"Okay, okay. I'll show you." I sat her down in her desk chair and stood in front of her with my hands stretched out, palms up. "Now I've discovered that there are two things I can do with my hands. First, I can make them pulse with heat. Feel my fingertips," I instructed her when they started to turn red and throb.

"Oh my God," she said after touching them quickly. "They've got to be like over a hundred degrees Celsius!"

"What does that mean?"

"One hundred degrees Celsius or 212 degrees Fahrenheit is the boiling point of water. Show me something else."

"Okay, for the next thing, I really have to concentrate. Just watch my fingers closely, especially my index finger." I closed my eyes and concentrated on that secret part of my brain. Then I felt the energy shoot out of my fingers.

"Holy hotdogs," she said softly like she was afraid that if she spoke too loud the fire would disappear.

I opened my eyes and saw that a small amber yellow flame hovered above each of my fingertips. The ones above my index fingers were the strongest and also had bits of blue and purple twinkling in them.

"I ... I ... I don't know what to say." Tai's eyes were wide with wonder. I was just happy she didn't look freaked out or scared like my dad did.

"What do you think this means?" I asked, shutting off the flame and rubbing my hands together. It still kind of stung a little. I hoped Tai could come up with a reasonable explanation for this and that it had nothing to do with aliens.

"I don't know, but I'm pretty sure it's not normal." Tai spun around in her chair and clicked on her computer. "I've been scouring the Internet ever since you told me about it, and I've found absolutely nothing else like your ... situation."

"Great. I *am* an alien." I flopped down on her bed.

"Alien? What makes you think that?"

"Nothing. Never mind," I said, not wanting to tell her about the strange conversation between my parents. I normally didn't keep secrets from Tai, but it was just too embarrassing to share.

"I don't think you're an alien," she said, making one final decisive click on the keyboard. She scooted her chair over and turned the screen slightly so I could see it.

On the screen was a Photoshopped image of me in a red spandex body suit with a cape.

"You think I'm a superhero?" I said unenthusiastically, examining the image.

"Yes, superhero!" she exclaimed. "Like in one of your comic books. I can't believe you haven't thought of that. Oh my God, this is awesome," she said, clapping her hands. "My best friend is a superhero."

Well, I guessed that made sense. It was actually kind of cool to think that I could be a superhero. But since I hadn't fallen into a vat of radioactive material or been bitten by a spider, the question remained, where did the powers come from? I could still be an alien.

"So what else can you do?" Tai asked, standing and offering the chair to me. She took a brush out of the drawer and started working on my hair. This was our little ritual. Normally, when we talked it was with a hairbrush and comb in each hand.

"What makes you think I can do anything else? Isn't the fire enough?"

"Wishful thinking, I guess. I just think it's so cool. I can't believe you have superpowers!"

"Well, there is something else I can do."

"I knew it. I knew you were holding out on me. What is it?" She spun me around in the chair to look at me.

"I can hear things."

"You mean like voices? In your head?" She scrunched her nose up just like she did whenever the school cafeteria served fish sticks.

"No, not like that. I'm not crazy. I can hear sounds like ... go in the hallway and whisper something into your hand."

Tai stepped outside. I rolled my eyes when she whispered her phrase. My best friend really was a nerd.

"Okay, what did I say?"

"You said, 'Force equals mass times acceleration.'"

"Holy hot dogs, that's awesome!"

I shrugged. The awesomeness of my powers was starting to wear off the more my parents' words sunk in. What if they really did send me away?

"What's the matter? Why do you look so forlorn?"

"What does that mean?"

"Depressed."

"I'm not *forlorn*." I had to think of something to get her mind off of my powers. Honestly, I was sick of them. "I'm just worried about what I'm going to wear to Spencer's house tonight."

"I almost forgot about that."

"He said you could come, too."

"Really? I can go? To Spencer's house? Spencer Callahan?" If she were the athletic type, she would have done a back flip right there in her room. "We gotta do our hair."

Tai dashed to the bathroom to turn on the flat iron, curling iron, crimper, and electric brush. We were looking at a four- or five-hour hair styling session, and I didn't mind at all. I didn't want to think about superpowers.

An hour later, we were so focused on the dozens of outfits lying around Tai's room that we nearly jumped out of our skin when her mom knocked on the door.

"Tai, Channel 2 is here," she said through the door.

"Oh, okay, Mom." Tai took slow, deep breaths. Suddenly, she looked like she might puke.

"Channel 2? Why is Channel 2 here?" I asked.

She sat down at her desk and took her Rock Box out of the drawer. For the most part, Tai was a perfect, charming, polite, beautiful genius. She was every parent's dream child, but she did have one strange little quirk. Whenever she got really nervous, she took out this shoe box full of rocks that she'd collected over the years. Then, one by one, she'd take them all out and then put them back in. She had a special order and rhythm to the process as well, and if she got thrown off or interrupted, she'd have to start all over again. Thankfully, by the time she was finished with her rock ritual, she always got back to normal.

The rock thing would've driven most people crazy. I mean, she could be at it anywhere from two minutes to two hours depending on what triggered it. But I just considered it a minor side effect to having such a great best friend.

"While I was at physics camp, I took this test and I did kinda well, so Channel 2 wants to do a story on me. No big deal," she said, focusing on her rocks.

It *was* a big deal. It was a huge deal. If it wasn't, she wouldn't be rubbing rocks as we spoke.

"Will you come with me? Will you sit with me?" she asked. Well, really, she pleaded.

"Tai, I wish I could, but my dad would flip if he found out I got on TV. You know how he is about privacy and keeping a low profile."

"Well, you wouldn't have to say anything. Just sit next to me. I could use the moral support." She scraped the rocks back into the box and started all over again. She was extremely nervous about this.

I really didn't want to do it, but how could I leave my best friend hanging? Over the years, my father had instilled in me his desire to stay out of the limelight at all costs. When I was little, I used to be really good at gymnastics. Getting up at 4:00 a.m. every day and driving to Pittsburgh for practice really paid off when I won the junior division title at eight years old. My coach said that if I kept training, I would probably make the Olympic team as a teenager. I was so excited. I could already see myself on the cover of a Wheaties box holding a gold medal. I thought Dad would be excited, too, but when I told him, he flipped out. He wouldn't even let the newspaper do a story on me because it meant my picture would be in it. And just like that, my gymnastics career ended because he thought it was too dangerous.

"Please, Priss. I don't think I can do this without you."

I sighed. "What if I sit off to the side so the camera doesn't see me."

"I guess that'll be okay."

* * *

"So tell us about the test. Was it hard?" Stacy Marguilles of Channel 2 News asked Tai while I stared at the two inches of makeup on the reporter's face. I mean, really she should've just put on a Halloween mask.

"It was a little challenging, but it was so much fun," Tai explained while I sat in the Houstons' brown wingback chair and stared at the orange shag carpeting. The Houstons hadn't redecorated since like the seventies. Every time I stepped into their house, I felt like I had jumped into an old rerun of Sesame Street. I didn't really understand what Mr. and Mrs. Houston did for a living. Basically, they got paid for being smart. They spent all their time reading big, fat, dusty books and then giving speeches about their findings. I don't know what possessed them to adopt a child. Don't get me wrong, I was glad that Tai came to River's Bend. I mean, she was my best friend in the world, the only person who really understood me. But Mr. and Mrs. Houston were a bit too old, formal, and stuffy to have kids. They were more likely to translate some ancient Egyptian manuscript than to play with their adopted daughter. They'd lived across the street from me my entire life and I didn't even know their first names.

"There was a section of chemistry on there that I wasn't familiar with, but since all the formulas were given, I was able to figure things out," Tai continued.

"That is simply amazing. So are you ready to go to Copenhagen to represent the U.S. in the international competition?"

Copenhagen? She was going to leave me again?

"I sure am. I can't wait."

"Well, it was certainly nice meeting you, Tai. You keep on making River's Bend proud." Stacy turned to the camera and said, "Tom, back to you."

"And we're out," the cameraman said. He took the camera off of his shoulder and whipped off his headphones while another man unhooked wires and started winding up the huge, thick cable that ran from the camera to the news truck outside.

"You're leaving the country? Why didn't you tell me about this?" I asked her once we were back in her room.

"I'm sorry I didn't tell you. I knew you wouldn't be happy with me. But it's only for a week this time."

I sat on her bed and pouted. This would be the fourth time this year she left me. I'd be stuck hanging out with Kyle again. Some best friend she was.

"I'll make it up to you, I promise." She sat down on the bed and put her arm around me. I shrugged her arm off my shoulder. "Look, you'll have plenty of time to hate me later. Right now, I have to get you ready for your date tonight."

She had a good point there.

Chapter 8

Girl Power

After Tai and I finished styling each other's hair, I went home to get dressed. On Tai's recommendation, I wore a green and brown summer dress that brought out the green in my eyes. It was the kind of dress that tied at the back of the neck and that required boobs to give the full effect, but a cute little brown shrug drew the attention away from my lack of upper body accessories.

All dressed and ready to go, I sat in my room trying to think of a way to get out of the house without having to tell my dad I was going to see a boy. Tai had it easy. Her parents trusted her so much that they basically let her do whatever she wanted. Mr. and Mrs. Houston were actually going to drop her off at Spencer's house. Ha! I could be thirty years old and married with three kids and my father still wouldn't hand me off to another man. I flopped back on my bed. It was hopeless.

Just then, I heard a knock on my door.

"Let's go," Josh said, poking his head in.

"Go where?" Didn't he know I had a date tonight? I wasn't going anywhere with him. Gosh, he could be so thick-headed.

"I'm taking you to the movies," he said, leaning into the hallway like he was looking for something … or someone.

"What are you talking about? I'm going to see Spencer tonight." I folded my arms and rolled my eyes at his stupidity.

"I know that, dummy!" he whispered, leaning back into my room. "I told Dad I was taking you to the movies. I'll drop you off at Spencer's then go pick up Stefanie."

Oh, wow, okay. That was actually pretty brilliant. I shrugged, grabbed my purse, and followed him into the kitchen.

After a million questions from my dad, including what movie we were seeing, the subject matter, the start time and end time, even the route we planned on taking to and from the theater, we were finally free to go. Serious overkill. I mean, there was only one theater in town, and just like everything else, it was on Main Street. River's Bend was so freaking small he could throw a rock up in the air in the middle of town square and it would have a 40 percent chance of hitting one of his own kids in the head.

Thankfully, Josh had answers to all the questions. He had really thought this through.

"Why are you doing this, Josh?" I asked once we were in his pickup truck.

He took out the ring he'd bought for Stefanie and held it in front of him. "You keep my secret, I'll keep yours."

Who would've thunk it. Me and Josh working together. It felt good to have an ally, especially since I no longer trusted my parents and my best friend always left town every time I turned around.

Most people in River's Bend had a huge house, but Spencer's was probably the hugest. Is that a word? Anyway, his front yard was literally a golf course. And his backyard looked like a postcard, complete with horses, ponds, and a cute little gazebo. The cool thing about the

Callahans was that they didn't act like rich people even though they were. They made their oldest son, Trevor, work during the summers to help pay for college, and Spencer shopped at thrift stores. From what I heard, the family didn't even spend money on Christmas gifts, but instead volunteered together at a soup kitchen in Pittsburgh. Spencer was definitely, without a doubt, my dream guy. Tonight was going to be perfect.

Thankfully, Josh drove me right up to the front door and I didn't have to make the half-mile trek from the main road.

"I'll pick you up at eight fifteen sharp."

"Eight fifteen? Can't I stay a little longer?"

"Eight fifteen is already pushing it, Priss. The movie we're supposed to be watching is over at seven thirty. Plus we have school tomorrow. Eight fifteen, and don't be late."

Josh put the car in gear and got ready to pull off, but I tapped on the door to make him stop, and said, "Thanks, Josh."

He smiled as he drove off. I really hoped Stefanie realized what a great guy she was getting.

I turned around to knock on the door, but before I could, it swung open.

"Hey, Priss. What's going on?" Spencer beamed at me with his gorgeous smile and electric eyes.

I loved that he said "what's going on" instead of "what's up." That was one of Tai's pet peeves. She always said "what's up" was a stupid question. Up is a direction not a state of being. Or something like that.

"Not much," I replied, trying to give my cutest smile. But he didn't even notice. He kind of looked past me down his mammoth driveway.

"I thought Tai was coming," he said.

"Oh, she is. We just didn't ride together."

"Okay, sweet. Well, Cali, Rebecca, and Helen are in the kitchen, making something called peppermint bark." He shrugged. "I don't know what it is, but it has something to do with chocolate so it's fine with me. Kyle, Ethan, and Manny are in the game room playing *Street Mania*. Just make yourself at home." He held the door open for me and let me enter. He didn't follow me into the house like I'd hoped. Instead, he stood by the door and continued looking out through the glass frame ...probably waiting for the rest of his guests.

I heard the girls giggling in the kitchen, but I was more drawn to the guys in the game room. I was an expert at *Street Mania*. Josh bought a copy of the racing game at the beginning of summer. When I first played against him, he beat me like a piñata, but I don't give up easily. I stayed up for twenty-four hours straight and played it constantly. The next day, I was able to keep up with him. After a month, I was beating him so badly that he didn't want to play it anymore.

That's the thing about me. I might not be as smart as Tai, but when I put my mind to it, I could conquer any challenge.

"Can I play?" I asked when I went into the huge game room complete with leather sofas and flat screen TV.

Ethan and Manny were so focused on their race that they didn't even realize someone had entered the room. Kyle rolled his eyes and said, "No way, Slumner. This game is boys only. Why don't you head off to the kitchen with the other girls?" Kyle waved his hand in the air and dismissed me as if I was a fly threatening his meal.

"What's the matter, Kyle? Afraid you'll lose to a girl … again?" I asked. That worked. I could basically get Kyle to do anything I wanted by threatening his manhood.

Twenty minutes later, I had beaten him four straight times. Not only did I beat him, I crushed him. What I did to that boy in that game bordered on child abuse, it was so devastating. Then I actually stood on the coffee table and, with my arms in the air, roared, "Girl power!"

Cali, Rebecca, and Helen came from the kitchen and joined in on the chanting. In the middle of our celebrating, I realized my best friend wasn't there to enjoy it with me. As a matter of fact, neither was Spencer. I hadn't seen him since I got there. I wasn't even sure if Tai had arrived.

I got down from the table and concentrated on finding her voice. When I did, I heard her laughing. I followed the sound to the gazebo out back. Tai and Spencer stood in the center of the gazebo as the sun hung just above the horizon behind them. Spencer was showing Tai his pet iguana, Scabby. She squealed and laughed each time he brought it close to her, refusing to actually touch it. Tai was not a lizard type of girl.

Why was Spencer showing Tai so much attention?

I ducked behind a bush and listened to their conversation.

"We should probably head back in. They can't possibly still be playing that game," Tai said.

"Ha, you don't know Kyle. We might just be here all night until he finally beats Priss. But I don't mind. I ... I like spending time with you."

"But, what about Priss?"

"What about her?"

"I thought you ... she said that ... I—"

"Look, Priss is cool, but it's you that I really wanted to see tonight."

"Me? Why?"

"Because I think you're incredible and beautiful and smart. And I ... I ... I'd really like to get to know you better."

My chest tightened. It hurt to breathe. I couldn't listen to them anymore. I ran away as fast as I could. I didn't know where I was going. I just ran. I ran faster and faster hoping that if I just concentrated on putting one foot in front of the other, I wouldn't notice my tears falling.

Chapter 9

The Great Mistake

Stupid! Stupid! Stupid! How could I possibly think he liked me? Of course he fell for Tai. She's so smart and so easy to talk to, not to mention completely adorable.

I ended up in the Callahans' horse stable, drying my tears with the cute little brown shrug that was supposed to attract Spencer's attention. After kicking a pail and sending it sailing across the room, I sank down into a pile of hay and tried to shut out all the sounds flooding my head. Suddenly, I heard everything everywhere. Okay, that's a slight exaggeration, but I heard sounds coming from Spencer's house as well as bits of conversations from passengers of cars driving on the main road. That had to be like two miles away!

My brain couldn't filter the sounds, giving me a massive headache. I felt hot and flushed everywhere. A strangely powerful hot flash was creeping up on me. My powers were completely out of whack. I thought I had learned to control them, but maybe I had gotten so emotional that I couldn't anymore.

I lifted my hands out of the hay, afraid that any second a spark would fly out and send the whole barn up in flames.

That thought scared me so much that I had to struggle more and more to keep the fire inside me. Then, just when I thought I couldn't take it anymore and I was about to literally burst into flames, that calm feeling settled over me. The same feeling I felt when I was in the Crawford bathroom. My breathing slowed down and I felt my head clear. I loved this feeling. It was like floating on a gentle breeze or sticking your head out of a car window on a cool November day.

What was going on with me? Was that another part of my powers? I could miraculously calm myself?

I didn't complain. Anything was better than that uncontrollable hot flash I had felt coming. That was a scary feeling.

I leaned my head against the wooden wall and thought about my sucky evening. I knew it wasn't Tai's fault that Spencer liked her instead of me, but I was still angry and hurt and just plain sad. Why did she have to be so cute? I closed my eyes and cried some more.

Josh will never know, a voice inside my head said.

Josh? Who cared about Josh right now? Wait, no. The voice didn't come from my head.

I wiped the tears from my face and concentrated on where the voice was coming from. I desperately wanted to think about something else besides Tai and Spencer. And this seemed like just the adventure I needed. Someone was talking about my brother. No one else named Josh lived in River's Bend.

I followed the voice to the guest house near the lake. Trevor usually stayed there when he was home from college. As I got closer, I noticed that Stefanie's car was parked behind it. What was she doing there? Wasn't she supposed to be somewhere getting a promise ring from my brother?

"Look, Stefanie, I don't think this is a good idea. Josh is a good guy. And you're a little young for me," Trevor was saying.

"You're nineteen; I'm seventeen. Nothing's wrong with that."

Ooh, what a little liar! She wouldn't be seventeen for three more months. I knew because Josh was already planning her surprise birthday party.

"Girls mature so much faster than boys, which means you and me are so much more compatible. Josh is a little boy. I need a man, like you."

Then I heard kissing sounds. Oh my God! Stefanie was cheating on Josh. This would crush him. This night was just getting worse and worse.

My anger grew as I thought about how Josh was going to feel. He was planning on proposing to that little skank. Hands on hips, I marched over to where her precious pink Pontiac was parked. I touched her tire and then sent a spark, instantly melting a hole into it. I repeated the process with the other three tires. Her stupid tacky car was now an immovable hunk of metal.

Well, really, all she needed to do is get four more tires and the car would be good as new. Just when I had decided to pop the hood and do a little more damage, I heard Josh's car in the distance. Well, actually, I heard a Christina Aguilera song getting louder and louder on a car radio and I assumed it was him. I turned out to be right.

I ran as fast as I could to Spencer's front door to meet him. I didn't want him to come looking for me and find Stefanie with Trevor. As I ran, I peeked at my watch. It was only 6:25. Why was he back so early?

By the time I reached the driveway, Josh was already out of the car and rushing to the front door. "Priss, get in the car. We gotta go," he yelled as soon as he saw me. He turned and hopped back into the driver's seat.

"Why? What's going on?" I asked, scrambling to get into the pickup before he drove off.

"You messed up, Priss. Big time."

Oh my God. What did I do? As Josh peeled out of Spencer's driveway, I racked my brain trying to figure out how I'd messed up. I couldn't think of anything. He couldn't have found out about me vandalizing Stefanie's car. Not that fast, anyway. Not unless he was psychic or something. And besides the waffle attack from the twins, things had been pretty calm at the Sumner house. It couldn't be what I had done to Chester. I'd already told dad I would make it up to him. I had no idea what this was about.

"How did I mess up, Josh? What did I do?"

"You mean you have no idea what this is about?" he asked as he ran a stop sign. I shook my head. "Think really, really hard about everything you did today."

I thought and thought, but I couldn't come up with anything.

"Josh, I really don't know. Just tell me."

"No, *you* tell me. Please tell me that you were not on the six o'clock news today along with Tai talking about some science test. Please say that it was some other skinny, big-mouthed, red-headed Priscilla Sumner."

I leaned forward and slammed my head against the dashboard. "Snap! I thought I stayed out of the camera shot."

"Well, you didn't. And now Dad's flipping out. He called the movie theater to find us. Good thing I was actually there. Stefanie wasn't home so I went to see a movie after all. Can you imagine what would've happened if I wasn't there?"

No, I couldn't imagine. Well, I could imagine, but I didn't want to. It would probably include my father running down the streets of River's Bend screaming our names at the top of his lungs. I shuddered at the possible embarrassment.

*   *   *

"What is this?" my dad barked, pointing to the TV screen as soon as Josh and I entered the house. On it was an image of me in the Houston living room. I guessed he had TiVo'd the news footage and paused where I had gotten on camera. The cameraman must have panned the living room while Tai was talking to the reporter. I hadn't even noticed. "What did I tell you about publicity?" he yelled at me.

"Daddy, I'm sorry. I didn't know I would get on TV. I tried to sit out of the camera's view." Then I started crying. I didn't know why I was crying. It didn't seem that important to me. But my father's yelling really scared me.

"Dad, what's the big deal?" Josh asked, hugging me. "It was local news. There's only like two thousand people in River's Bend and they all know Priss by name. This town is so small they probably know her favorite color and shoe size as well. Why are you freaking out?"

I buried my face in Josh's chest. Thankfully, he had a shirt on. My dad didn't respond. I heard his big feet pounding the wooden floor as he paced the living room. I wiped my tears and looked at him. He stopped pacing, shut his eyes tightly, and then took a deep breath.

"I'm sorry. I'm so sorry for yelling at you." He wrapped his arms around Josh and me and nearly lifted us off the ground. He hugged us so tightly I started to run out of air. "I just love you so much. I don't know what I'd do if anything happened to you."

"Like what?" Josh asked, pushing away from the group hug.

"I don't know. Anything," my dad said. He let me go and headed toward the basement.

"Oh no you don't." Josh ran to block his path. "You *do* know. There's some reason why you're so paranoid. It's not normal that you time us everywhere we go, that we're not allowed to have yearbook pictures or cell phones, and that I've lived in this house for sixteen years and have never been in that basement."

My father arched his shoulders back and puffed his chest out. He looked huge, massive, colossal. For a moment I thought Josh would lose his resolve and run away. I certainly wanted to. But no, Josh stood his ground. He wanted answers.

When he realized Josh wasn't moving, Dad softened and said, "Have a seat on the couch. Both of you." He rubbed his shaved head while walking back and forth in front of us, trying to find the right words. "Your mother's job is very dangerous. Life-and-death dangerous," he said finally. "I'm constantly afraid that someone will come after one of you in retaliation against her, especially you, Priscilla. You look so much like your mother, anyone could take one look at you and know you were Quindolyn's child."

That was enough information for me. My mother had a dangerous job and people wanted to kill her. I got it. Dad was trying to protect us. Conversation over. I just wanted to go to my room and cry while trying to forget this night ever happened. Josh wasn't satisfied, though.

"That's not good enough. There's more to it. What could possibly be so dangerous about working for a pharmaceutical company?" Josh stood, challenging my father again.

"Joshua Allen Sumner," my father said in that low, scary parent voice that's even scarier than the loud yelling voice. The voice that says they mean business and they're going to explode if you push them any further.

"I've said all I'm going to say tonight. Now go to your room."

Josh's eyes expanded. He knew my father had reached his limit. "I hate this house!" he yelled, storming to his room.

When my father's eyes landed on me, I hopped up and dashed to my room as well. I certainly wasn't going to ask him any more questions. And I definitely wasn't going to tell him anything about my hot flashes. I didn't know how he would react. Would he be the loving father who didn't care if we saw him cry? Or would he be the big, scary, kill-you-with-one-look father who I had just seen?

I wasn't taking any chances. My fire-shooting fingers would be my secret forever.

Chapter 10

First Day of School

Tai and I used to have a first-day-of-school ritual. We would meet in front of her house and then walk to Willy's Sweet Shop for a lemonade and a cinnamon roll. After staying up half the night deciding what outfit to wear on the first day of school, we usually needed the sugar rush to get us going. Then we would plan out our day as we walked. This usually meant we figured out times and places to meet to talk about Spencer sightings.

This year was different in more ways than one. First of all, we didn't stay up the night before discussing wardrobe possibilities. I didn't even return her three phone calls. Second of all, Tai would be taking eighth grade classes, which meant I would see her even less than normal. They wanted her to go right into high school this year, but she refused because she didn't want to leave her friends behind. And third, I doubted we would meet to talk about Spencer. He was the last thing I wanted to think about.

After last night, I didn't want to walk to school with Tai. I stared out of my window and saw her standing at the corner waiting for me, looking way too cute in her lavender tank top and matching lavender and black pleated skirt. She rocked back and forth on her heels while looking up and down the street. Her eyes fell on my house several times. I felt like a part of me was missing. I didn't know if I knew how to be Priss without Tai by my side. Even while she was away at camp, we talked on the phone three or four times a day. Who would I talk to now?

Just when I was about to turn away from the window and sneak out the back door of my house, I saw Spencer come up to Tai on his skateboard.

"You want to walk to school together?" he asked her. What a stupid question. He could've been at school ten minutes ago. He had to pass Polk Middle to get from his house to Tai's house. Wait a minute. I guess that's how much he liked her. He went out of his way to walk with her.

"I don't think so," Tai said, looking at my house. "I'm waiting for Priss. We always walk to school together."

"Well, the bell's going to ring in a few minutes. You're gonna be late if you wait any longer."

Tai looked at her watch and then looked at my house again. She shrugged her shoulders and sighed. "Okay."

* * *

"You look terrible," Kyle said to me while I loaded my locker with books.

In third grade Kyle said my hair color reminded him of something that his dog threw up. When I started crying, Spencer came to my defense and told Kyle that he should probably take his dog to the vet because that didn't sound healthy. That was when I fell in love with Spencer and when Kyle kind of fell off my radar. Normally, I just ignored his insensitive remarks, but he chose the wrong day to mess with me. I was not having it.

"How dare you say something like that to me, you conceited, inconsiderate, little turd! Just because I don't get paid to smile in front of a camera doesn't mean you can comment on my looks. You've got some nerve, Kyle Montgomery." I poked him in the chest with my finger, making him back up and slam against the lockers. People in the hallway turned and stared at us. "You apologize to me right now or you're gonna regret it." I was so hot I probably burned a hole in his shirt with my finger.

Kyle looked absolutely terrified. His mouth opened and closed, searching for words, and his hands were shaking, literally shaking.

"I ... I ... I'm sorry, Priss. I really am. I didn't mean it like that. I just meant you looked sad. You look like you've lost your best friend or something."

Did it show that much? It had only been sixteen hours since I last talked to Tai, and already a self-centered egomaniac like Kyle noticed something was wrong with me. How was I ever going to get through this?

To make matters worse, my favorite teacher, Mr. Billings, didn't come back to teach math. Mr. Billings never made me feel stupid in class and always said that the answer was in me; I just had to get it out. Sometimes he would even put on music and let us try to shake the right answer out. I usually still got the answer wrong, but at least I didn't dread going to math class.

Mr. Billings apparently retired yesterday and his replacement, Mr. Witherall, was just plain creepy. He had a face that looked like plastic. The same blank expression was glued to it all the time, and I never knew if he was happy or sad or even breathing. It was like getting taught by a mannequin. And to top it all off, he had a glass eye. Or at least I think it was glass. I wasn't sure. I just knew it didn't move with the other eye, which creeped me out so much it gave me shivers just thinking about it. *I'll have to ask Tai about glass eyes and … wait a minute.* I'm not *talking to Tai.* Ugh, my life sucked.

"I hope you have a good day," he said in his deep raspy voice when class was over. He sounded like he was eighty years old but he looked about my parents' age. I wondered if he'd had surgery and that's why his face looked so fake. I could tell he was trying to look younger than his age the way his hair was dyed an unnatural shade of black.

I looked around the classroom to make sure he was talking to me since I couldn't really tell who or what he was looking at.

"Yes, I'm talking to you, Priscilla." That made sense. I was the only one left in the room.

"How do you know my name?"

"I have the class roster. I know all of your names."

"Yeah, but it usually takes new teachers a few days to learn everyone."

"Well, you stand out, Priscilla."

I didn't like the way he said my name. He said it slow and dragged out the S sound. It gave me a weird feeling.

I grabbed my books and high-tailed it out of there. I made a mental note to never be alone with that weird guy again.

* * *

I knew I was supposed to take the twins to the park that afternoon to make up for what I had done to Chester, but I was already in a sucky mood and I didn't feel like walking to the park. I was too tired after my stressful day. So, instead, I dressed them in their swim trunks, took them to the side yard, and pointed a water hose at them. They loved it, and I didn't have to get out of my lawn chair.

While the devil twins laughed and giggled in the water, I stared down the street at Tai's house. I wondered if she was home. Did she find her eighth grade classes hard? Maybe she was still at school, studying. I had done such a good job of avoiding her all day that I kinda hoped she'd step out of the house for a second just so I could get a glimpse of her. I shook my head. What a pathetic thought. I didn't need a best friend. I would be just fine by myself.

I turned my back on the Houston house so I could concentrate on the devil twins, but ... they weren't there.

"Charlie, Chester!" I yelled franticly. "Where are you?" There was no telling what those little trouble makers were getting into. Dad would kill me if something happened to them because I wasn't paying attention. I closed my eyes and tried to listen for their voices but couldn't hear anything. That was bad. They were never quiet.

"If Prissy won't take us to the park, we can take ourselves. I'll get the car," I heard Chester whisper.

What car?

"I'll make sure no one sees," Charlie said. I ran to the front of the house and saw Charlie standing in the driveway. Chester was in the driver's seat of Dad's Escalade. And it was moving. Chester had gotten it into neutral. The driveway was slanted just enough for it to start rolling back, right toward Charlie.

I ran as fast as I could. If I hurried, I would be able to push Charlie out of the way in time. Suddenly, I was falling. My face hit the dirt with a thud. I had tripped over one of Charlie's toy trucks. As I scrambled to my feet, I saw the massive SUV barreling down on my baby brother. There was no way I could get there in time. The car was a second away from impact.

Without thinking, I leaped up, lunged for the car, and grabbed hold of the front tire on the driver's side. Amazingly, it stopped. I had stopped a car just by holding the tire.

Chester jumped out of the front seat, and he and Charlie ran into the house, laughing up a storm. Afraid to move, I stared at my hands gripping the tire. How was I strong enough to hold an Escalade in place? It had to be another part of my powers. This wasn't normal. I had to get this car back into place before someone saw me. Slowly, I got to my feet without letting go of the tire. I grabbed the open driver's side door, hopped in, and then quickly put it in park. Crisis averted.

Tai had told me once about this woman who was able to lift a car to get it off of her child. She said that the adrenaline had momentarily given her super strength. I wondered if that was the case with me. Did I just have a momentary burst of strength because I wanted to save Charlie? Or did I really have super strength? I had to know.

I jumped out of the car and then stepped around to the front of it. I made sure no one was watching and grabbed hold of the front fender. Then, with just one finger, I pulled the car forward toward the garage. Now *that's* girl power!

Chapter 11

Snot Wars

Thursday morning I woke up looking forward to using my fingers to make a nice warm bath, but something felt different in my body. My powers were gone. I tried to listen for Josh singing in the shower, but I couldn't hear a thing, thank God. I tried to make heat rise from my fingertips. Nothing. Finally, I got out of bed and tried to lift it with one hand. It wouldn't budge. A feeling of relief washed over me. A part of me would miss my powers. I was glad I had them when I needed to save Charlie's life. I'd had a couple of nightmares imagining what would have happened if the car had hit him. All joking aside, I kinda loved my brothers.

I didn't know where the powers came from or why they had disappeared. Maybe it was just part of some divine fluke that was meant for me to save my brother's life. I didn't know and I didn't care. I was just glad they were gone. It was a burden having a secret like that. There was no one I could trust. I was just glad Tai hadn't told anyone. Or, at least I hoped she hadn't.

Things were still super weird between Tai and me. I hadn't spoken to her since that night at Spencer's house. Come to think of it, I hadn't addressed another issue of betrayal that came up that night.

No matter how hard I tried, I couldn't gather up enough courage to tell Josh about Stefanie. I kinda hoped that he would realize on his own what an awful person she was and dump her. But that didn't happen. In fact, I came home to find the bottle-blonde, bubble-blowing, lying, little bimbo sitting on my couch and staring at her new ring. It was the promise ring that Josh wanted to give her. I felt a heat rising in me. I wanted to set her face on fire. I know that's mean, but she was really going to break my brother's heart. I couldn't let her do it.

I had to tell Josh the truth. But would he even believe me? And if he did, what if he ended up hating me? I sucked in a deep breath and decided it had to be done.

"Hey, Patricia," Stefanie said as I walked past where she was perched on our couch. Dad would flip if he saw her feet up on the coffee table. He had just dusted it. Thankfully, he was at the grocery store.

"It's Priscilla," I said even though I kinda thought she already knew that and just called me Patricia to annoy me.

"Whatever. Could you just tell your brother to bring me an iced tea with my sandwich? Thanks a bunch." Then she pulled her gum out of her mouth, wrapped it around her finger, plopped it back in, and blew a bubble. If there were bubble gum Olympics, she would win a gold medal, hands down.

"How's your car?" I asked as nicely as I could, showing off a fake smile.

"What do you know about that?"

"Oh, just that tires can be expensive nowadays."

She stopped smacking and glared at me, her eyes turning to slits. Then she smiled and resumed her brutal assault on that poor, defenseless gum before saying, "No matter. Josh bought new tires for me."

I gasped. My brother actually paid for her tires? Poor Josh was paying in more ways than one for her lying and cheating. He'd been saving his money for over a year to pay for a football camp at Penn State. He'd probably spent all his money on those tires. This was the last straw. Oh, this chick was going down. I stormed into the kitchen and found my brother making Stefanie's favorite sandwich: turkey, roast beef, and Swiss cheese on rye bread with the edges cut off and a smidge of low-fat mayonnaise. I was annoyed that I even knew that.

"Josh, there's something you need to know about Stefanie."

"I know, I know. Iced tea." He grabbed a Snapple out of the fridge as if he was in a hurry. God forbid the skank have to wait for her sandwich.

"No, not that." I took a deep breath and blurted, "Stefanie's cheating on you with Trevor Callahan."

"That's not possible. Trevor's in college. He already went back to Duquesne." Josh didn't even pause in his sandwich preparation.

"I know, but before he left, he was kissing Stefanie. It was on Labor Day."

"I don't know where you're getting this from or why you would make this up, but Stefanie wouldn't do that to me. She's wearing my ring."

"Josh!" Stefanie called from the living room.

"Coming, babe." Josh poured the Snapple into a glass and placed it on a tray next to Stefanie's sandwich. "Priss, we'll talk about this later. But you need to learn to like Stefanie. She's going to be your sister one day."

I almost puked.

Josh obviously needed more proof. And I needed reinforcements in order to get it. Just then, the devil twins ran through the kitchen, each sporting freshly painted green hair. I didn't know why their hair was green and I didn't care. I just needed their help.

I stopped them both, holding them by their collars so they wouldn't run off.

"You guys up for a game?"

For the past year or so, Charlie and Chester had perfected a game they liked to call Snot Wars. Basically, they earned points for hitting certain predetermined targets with none other than their very own snot. Yes, they would press one nostril closed and then, after taking a deep breath, aim a snot rocket at an inanimate target. We had to limit the boys to inanimate objects after Max Montgomery ran away from being the victim of one too many snot attacks. I don't know where they got an endless supply of snot from, but I swear, I've seen Charlie hit a lamp shade from ten feet away.

Josh and I kept our belongings safe by telling the twins that if any snot ever fell on any of our stuff, they'd earn negative points. That was enough. They were so into their game that they had their own scoring system. Right now Charlie had forty hundred gazillion trillion points, and Chester had thirty fifteen hundred million bazillion points. I wasn't sure who was winning.

Given the fact that Stefanie was in the local newspaper for sending ten thousand text messages in the month of July alone, I just assumed that she would have some little love notes written to Trevor on her annoyingly pink sparkly Blackberry.

In order to distract Stefanie long enough for me to snatch her phone, I told the twins that there was a target in the house worth a hundred billion trillion gazillion points. The target: Stefanie's mouth.

Josh knew something was going on when he saw the twins skulking around the living room in their blue camouflage Osh Kosh B'Gosh overalls. They were stalking their prey. I guess I should've told them that the war paint was unnecessary.

"Priss, get the twins out of here. They're up to something," Josh called while wrapping a protective arm around his girlfriend.

"What? They can't play in their own house? They're fine." I peeked into the living room from the hallway and noticed that Chester and Charlie had worked out an attack plan through a series of hand signals. Charlie was going to distract Josh while Chester went in for the first shot.

Charlie dug a half-eaten Twinkie out of his pocket and lobbed it at Josh. Josh leaped off of the couch and charged after him. But little Charlie was quick. As Josh's pursuit of the Twinkie-thrower spilled out into the backyard, Chester jumped on the coffee table, closed a nostril, aimed, and fired.

Stefanie's wild screams filled the house as she manically wiped snot off of her forehead. She shot off the couch and ran to the bathroom, giving me the opportunity to rifle through her purse. Once I had the phone in my hand, I ducked into a corner and scrolled through her text messages.

"What's going on? Why is Stefanie screaming?" Josh asked, bursting back into the house.

"I missed." Chester poked out his lip, crossed his arms, and flopped into a chair.

"Missed? Missed what? Oh God, not Snot Wars." Josh ran to the bathroom to find Stefanie.

Seconds later, Josh emerged from the bathroom and screamed, "I'm gonna kill you, Chester!"

"Josh, wait," I said, stepping in front of him. "He's not the one you should be mad at." I held up the phone as he started reading countless text messages from Stefanie to Trevor, or as she put it "Sexy Trevy."

"I hope you're going to punish that little beast!" Stefanie yelled when she came out of the bathroom.

Josh didn't respond to that request. Instead, he silently handed over her phone and said, "How could you?" before sulking off to his room.

Stefanie's mouth flew open, giving Charlie the perfect opportunity. He won the hundred billion trillion gazillion points.

Chapter 12

The Painful Pen

Josh didn't come out of his room for two days. I felt really bad for him. I offered to let him win at *Street Mania*, but he wasn't interested. I tried to tell him I knew how he felt. I mean, I had not only lost the love of my life, but my best friend, too. But I wasn't really ready to talk about that situation. Especially after what happened a few days later.

I was sitting in English class, trying to stuff an X-Men comic into my literature book so that I could read something interesting during class, when Spencer took a seat next to me. I had to admit, my heartbeat started to race. I mean, even though he had rejected me for Tai and we hadn't spoken since his Labor Day party, it didn't make him any less cute.

"Hey, Priss," he whispered, leaning toward me. This was supposed to be quiet reading time. I loved this part of class because I got to relax in a bean bag and forget about my worries. And I had a lot of worries lately.

"Hi, Spencer," I whispered back.

He didn't speak for a few minutes as he focused on his *Chronicles of Narnia* book. But I could tell he wanted to say something the way he flipped back and forth between the same two pages. I watched him out of the corner of my eye. He was wearing a faded red Van Halen t-shirt and a pair of raggedy, holey jeans. He looked amazing.

"Are you going to the River Day Dance?" he asked finally, staring at me through his shaggy hair that hung over his eyes. The River Day Dance was a stupid town tradition in which we were supposed to dress up like pilgrims or something and celebrate the founding of the town. The only people who ended up dressing up were the over-sixty crowd. The young people usually ditched the festivities and went home to watch TV. The only time it was worthwhile going to the River Day Dance was if you had a date and you were in love. In that case, it was really old-fashioned and romantic.

"Um, I don't know. Maybe." I shifted nervously in my seat. Maybe Spencer realized he loved me instead of Tai. Maybe he was about to ask me to the River Day Dance.

"I asked Tai," he said, dashing my hopes and crushing my spirit once again. I just wanted to jump up and run out of the classroom, but my butt was kind of stuck in the bean bag chair. After two attempts at trying to hop up, I gave up and flopped back down. Spencer didn't notice my difficulty. Instead, he said, "She said no. She doesn't want to go to the dance with me."

I thought I noticed a tinge of hurt in his voice. He didn't look at me. He just kept absentmindedly flipping pages in his book.

"Sorry," I said with a shrug. I felt bad that I didn't really feel bad. So what if Tai didn't want to go to the dance with him? What did he want me to do about it?

Spencer closed his book, turned to me, and said, "Look, I know you two are tight. Do you think you can talk to her and find out why? I mean, she won't talk to me. I think I did something wrong but I don't know what. Can you just tell her I'm sorry?"

Oh his eyes were amazing. They were even more gorgeous when they were filled with love. Why couldn't that love be for me?

I knew what he had done wrong. He had fallen for the wrong girl. Tai would probably never go out with him because she knew it would hurt my feelings. I felt terrible. My selfishness was getting in the way of their happiness. I was so lost in my thoughts, I barely noticed when Spencer left and Kyle sat down in his place.

"Remember in the third grade when I said something about your hair color?" he whispered to me.

I nodded.

"I didn't mean to hurt your feelings. I actually liked your hair color. I just didn't know how to tell you. I … I … I still like your hair color."

I looked over at Kyle sitting cross-legged on the floor next to me. He had a first-edition Incredible Hulk comic stuffed into his book, but he'd chosen the wrong size book, and the edges of the comic poked out. He was sure to be caught by Mrs. Talendy.

"If Spencer doesn't like you, he's an idiot and it's his loss," he added. "You're the greatest girl ever. I'm sure you'll get a date to the dance."

Before I could say anything, he got up, tucked his book and comic under his arm, and scurried to the other side of the room. Why was he being so nice to me? I must have been really pathetic for Kyle Montgomery to actually feel pity for me. Was it that obvious how I felt about Spencer? Or maybe Tai had told him everything.

"Tai told me everything," Kyle said outside of math class two weeks later. He had gotten in the habit of following me around everywhere and asking me stupid questions like could he carry my books and what type of candy did I like. Ugh. Boys could be so weird sometimes. Since Tai and I weren't friends anymore, I just let him hang around so I wouldn't have to be alone.

"Everything about what?" I was so nervous I dropped my math book. Kyle scrambled to pick it up for me. I knew it! That little traitor had pulled a Lando Calrissian on me. She'd turned against me just like Lando turned against Han Solo in *Return of the Jedi*. If she told him about my powers, then soon the whole school would learn how she got so scared at the fourth grade camping trip that she peed in her sleeping bag and had to share mine. I had tons of secrets on her and I wasn't afraid to use them.

"She told me that it's her fault you two aren't talking but that you won't give her a chance to apologize." Instead of handing me back my math book, he tucked it under his arm and then held the door open for me so I could enter the classroom.

"She said that?" I flopped down in my favorite seat in the back. It was the desk right behind Susie Chambers whose head was so big she nearly completely hid me from Mr. Witherall's wandering glass eye. "Did she really say that?"

Kyle nodded as he took the seat next to me and placed my book on my desk. I sighed and slid down into my seat. I felt so guilty about not talking to Tai for twenty-four days. It wasn't really her fault. How could I blame her for how Spencer felt? After four years of friendship, I was willing to let a stupid boy get in the way.

I spent most of class thinking about what I could say to Tai to get our friendship back on track when suddenly, "Priscilla," Mr. Witherall called in his creepy, deep, raspy voice. "I asked you a question." Oh snap! Did he really ask me a question? I was totally not paying attention. I looked at Kyle for help. Maybe he could tell me the answer or at least the question. But Kyle just shrugged as he mouthed, "Sorry." He wasn't paying attention either. His hands were under his desk playing a game on his iPhone.

Not knowing what else to do, I yelled out, "Seven."

Everyone laughed. Apparently that wasn't the answer.

"No, Priscilla," he said, shaking his head in that teacher way that translated into "I really don't get paid enough for this."

"I asked you to come to the board."

"Oh, yeah, I knew that." I scooted out of my desk and made my way to the Smart Board, which was what Mr. Witherall used to teach class. The computerized pen along with the special screen allowed him to animate problems and stuff to make class more interesting. It didn't work. Stepping into his class was getting into a boxing ring with sleep as my opponent. Sleep usually won. And I always wondered, if the board was so smart, why did we need a teacher?

The pen felt heavy in my hands, and after I held it for a few seconds, it sent a surge of energy through me that was so painful I had to drop it. "Ouch!" I yelled.

"Oh, I'm sorry. It must have a short in the wiring or something," Mr. Witherall said casually as if he really wasn't sorry at all. He picked up the pen and pressed a couple of buttons on it. Just then the bell rang, ending class. "Okay, students, do the problems on page forty-three for tomorrow."

As everyone filed out of the classroom, I kept my eyes on that pen. If there was a short in the wiring or something, how come it had never shocked him? Then I noticed that he put the pen in a drawer and locked it before hurrying out of the classroom. Why didn't he put it in the holder on the side of the screen like he always did?

"Did you see that?" I asked Kyle as he packed up his backpack.

"See what?"

"Mr. Witherall put the pen that shocked me in a drawer." I was still rubbing the pain out of my hand. It felt like the electricity went straight to my bones.

"So?" he asked.

"So, isn't that weird?"

He shrugged. "Maybe he doesn't want anyone else to get hurt by it."

"Maybe." I thought about that for a second and then said, "But it didn't shock him. As a matter of fact, it hasn't ever shocked anyone. I don't know. I just have a weird feeling about it."

Kyle shrugged again. He just didn't get it. "Uh, it's lunch time now. Do you want to sit with me?"

"Nah, I'm not really hungry," I said, staring at the drawer where the evil, painful pen had gone. After a few seconds I realized Kyle was still standing next to me.

He tossed his backpack over his shoulder and stared at the ground. After running his fingers through his sun-bleached hair, he said, "I have a photo shoot in New York this weekend, but I thought that when I get back we could get together and play *Street Mania* or something. I've been practicing."

"Yeah, sure, whatever," I said, just wishing he would leave so I could get into that drawer with the pen.

"Great! I'll call you Sunday. Is it okay if I call you?"

"Yeah, sure, whatever."

"Great! Bye, Priss." Kyle dashed out of the room, leaving me alone with my thoughts. I had to figure out a way to get into that drawer and study that pen. But what good would it do for me to look at it? What were the chances I would understand it? I needed someone who was good with technology. Someone smart. Someone I could trust. I needed my best friend. I needed Tai.

Chapter 13

Kyle Loves PMS

The next day, I found Tai sitting in a swing on the playground during lunch.

"Hey," I said, jamming my hands in my jeans and kicking an invisible stone.

"Hey." Tai took out a napkin, placed her sandwich into it, and neatly folded it up. I guessed the sight of me made her lose her appetite.

"Why aren't you eating with the eighth graders?" The eighth grade students of Polk Middle had the best spot in the cafeteria: the three tables right in front of the soft serve ice cream machine. Basically, no one else got ice cream unless they were approved by an eighth grader or won the Ice Cream Challenge. Last year, Tai and I used to dream about being invited to sit with them. Sixth graders got laughed at if they even attempted to go near the ice cream machine. Seventh graders got invited once in a while, but now that Tai was technically an eighth grader, she should've been able to sit there without an invite. She should've been stuffing her face with ice cream instead of sitting alone in a swing set.

Tai shrugged. "They say even though I'm in their class that I'm still a seventh grader and I haven't earned the privilege."

"Well that's ridiculous," I said, crossing my arms. "If you've earned the right to take classes with them, then you've earned the right to eat their stupid ice cream. It's not their machine, anyway. They don't own it."

A silence exploded between us as Tai played with a string on her peach floral skirt and I twisted my hair around my finger. I didn't know what else to say. Well, I knew I needed to apologize, but saying sorry is a very hard thing to do. The words kept getting caught in my throat.

"Have you noticed I'm the only black person in town?" she said finally, breaking the silence.

I nodded. "So? I think that's cool. You're unique."

"I'm the only seventh grader taking eighth grade classes. I'm the only twelve-year-old and the only girl on the U.S. science bowl team."

"So?"

She sighed heavily and her shoulders sagged as she stared at her feet and clicked her black Mary Jane shoes. "I'm sitting in the playground eating a homemade turkey sandwich by myself, because I have no friends and everyone thinks I'm some sort of genius freak."

I finally started to understand where she was coming from.

"I'm a weird outcast. You're the only friend I have ... or had. Even my parents don't have time for me. I just wanted to be your friend, not the 'brilliant black girl from the Bend.'" Tai's lip quivered and she wiped away a tear.

Now I felt even worse. She thought I was her only friend and I had cast her aside over a stupid boy. Tai felt completely alone in the world. It was true that there was no one else like her. But was that a bad thing? I was pretty sure there was no one else in the world that could shoot fire from her fingers. We could be lonely freaks together.

A knot developed in my throat. Before I knew it, it was hard for me to see through the tears.

"I've been a complete and total jerk," I choked out. "I'll understand if you never want to talk to me again. I'm so sorry, Tai."

"I'm sorry, too," she said even though she really didn't need to apologize. She jumped out of the swing, dropping her sandwich in the dirt and tackling me with a hug. We both sobbed so much we kinda had to hold each other up.

"Let's never fight again," I said once I could catch my breath.

"Deal."

"Best friends forever."

"Forever."

When our simultaneous crying fits ended, we sat side by side on the swings and gabbed at break-neck speed about what had happened in our lives over the past few weeks. We had so much to say to each other that I almost forgot about the painful pen. "Wait a minute," I said, interrupting her telling me how she refused to go to the River Day Dance with Spencer. "I almost forgot. I need your help with something. Follow me." On the way to Mr. Witherall's classroom, I told her about the pen and how it shocked only me and how he then locked it away instead of putting it where he always kept it.

"That's weird," she said as we entered the seventh grade building.

"That's what I said, but Kyle didn't see anything wrong with it."

"Kyle, huh?" Tai had this smirk on her face like she knew something that I didn't.

"Yeah, Kyle, what about him?"

"You've been spending a lot of time with him, huh?" Tai said with a laugh.

"What's so funny?"

"I didn't think it was true, but I guess it is."

"What? You didn't think what was true?"

Tai smiled and said, "Kyle has 'I Love PMS' written on the inside of his locker."

"He loves PMS? Well, that's just stupid. Boys don't get a period."

"No, not that kind of PMS." Tai clutched her stomach, laughing so hard tears streamed down her face.

"Polk Middle School?"

"No, silly. Priscilla Maxine Sumner. P-M-S. He's in love with you!"

"Me? That's ridiculous. Kyle Montgomery doesn't love anyone but himself."

"Well, he must see a lot of himself in you."

"Whoa. Wait. What?" I shuddered at the thought. Kyle was a self-centered, egotistical, rude, insensitive jerk. We had absolutely nothing in common except that we both hated math class and loved racing up and down Main Street on our bikes. And two days ago we did spend an hour making a list of the top ten best comic book villains. And although every once in a while he said something stupidly mean, he always took it back and apologized when I brought it to his attention.

As we walked down the hall, Tai kept chattering on about some awesome program she wrote on her calculator, but I couldn't even pretend to be interested. All I could think about was Kyle. Who knew? Maybe he was turning into a decent person. When we reached the classroom I closed my eyes and tried to shake thoughts of Kyle out of my mind. I needed to concentrate on the mission at hand.

After making sure Mr. Witherall wasn't around, we entered the room and then stared at the desk that held the evil pen. It was a standard work desk with two file drawers on the right side. The top one was unlocked and opened easily. The bottom drawer was the one that had the pen, and it wouldn't budge.

"Okay, I know how we can get in," Tai said. "My friend, Luke, who went to camp with me in Florida created this 'key of all keys.' You insert a wire shell into the key hole then use a computer program to manipulate the wire to the right fit. Then voila, the lock opens. I can have him FedEx it to us and we can have it by Monday."

"Or," I said, yanking the drawer above the locked drawer completely out of the desk. "My parents have a desk just like this in the living room. They lock candy in it, thinking we can't get to it. The twins figured out that you can just pull out the top drawer to get to the bottom one."

Tai shrugged. "That works."

I pointed inside the desk. Tai looked and had a clear view of everything that was in the bottom drawer, including the pen. I reached for it and then hesitated, remembering the pain it had caused me.

"You get it," I said.

Tai shrugged and reached through the desk for the pen. Turning it around and around in her hands, I could almost see the calculations working out in her head. She was fascinated by the painful pen.

"What? What is it?" I asked, growing impatient.

"I've never seen anything like it. You see this here?" She pointed to the side of the pen. "That's a wireless antenna. I'm guessing it has a frequency strong enough to send information across the country."

"Why would a pen need to do that?"

"And you see this?" she asked, ignoring my question. "This is a USB port. I should be able to connect it to a computer and download whatever information it has."

"What kind of information do you think it has?"

Tai was silent for a moment. She scrunched up her face like she did whenever she had to do the rope climb in PE. "Let me see your hand," she said finally. "Just like I thought," she said after examining my hand. "The pen stuck you with a probe right there below your thumb. I think it took a sample of your skin or blood or something, and then it sent the information somewhere else, probably to a laboratory or something."

"Or to another planet. It was an alien probe, wasn't it? You can tell me. I knew I was an alien."

"Why do you think you're an alien?"

I quickly explained to her the conversation between my parents as she took out a calculator and some cords from her purse.

"Well, I guess anything's possible," she said when I finished. "But let's not jump to conclusions. Let's be rational about this." She connected her calculator to the pen and then punched some buttons. "There, that should do it." She yanked out the cords and shoved her calculator back into her purse. "Let's get this place cleaned up and get out of here. We don't want Mr. Witherall to catch us."

We put the pen back where we found it and closed up the desk. Just then, the bell rang, ending lunch.

"I downloaded all the information from the pen onto my calculator. I have Computer Science later today, so I should be able to decipher all the information and maybe even print out some stuff. Let's meet after school at Willie's and I'll tell you what I've found."

The next three hours were torture. I couldn't concentrate on anything. I kinda wished Kyle was still around so he could distract me with an in-depth conversation about the Batmobile or something, but he'd already left to catch a flight to New York. My stomach turned at the thought that I actually missed him. I almost puked.

The more I stared at the clock in Mrs. Talendy's class, the slower the hands moved. At one point I think they even went backward. But finally, it was all over. I jumped on my bike and pedaled over to Willie's Sweet Shop to wait for Tai. To pass the time, I bought a couple of raspberry cream lollipops for us. They were my absolute favorite candy in the world. They tasted like heaven on a stick.

Tai took so long, I ended up eating mine and hers. I paced up and down the aisles for a while, studying the pastries, the candies, and the ice creams as if I had not been to the shop practically every day of my life. Twenty minutes later, I really started to worry. I had already used

Willie's phone twice to call my dad and let him know where I was.

What was taking her so long? Then I had a scary thought. What if Mr. Witherall had found out about our snooping? What if he had captured her and kidnapped her and taken her to some evil place? My friend was in danger! I took a deep breath and tried to calm down. Life was not a comic book. I was totally overreacting. But I still made a mental note of what I would do to Mr. Witherall if he ever hurt my friend. And it wasn't pretty. His glass eye would be his most attractive feature when I was done with him.

Finally, I saw Tai running up to the store, clutching a large envelope to her chest. She burst through the door, sat down across from me at our favorite round wicker table, and said, "Sorry I'm late. It took me forever to break through the encryptions and find these." She dumped out the contents of the envelope onto the table. "There were several documents that I didn't understand, so I focused on the pictures."

"What the heck is going on?" I said as I stared at several pictures of me in hospital beds. "I've never been in the hospital."

"No, Priss, look at the time stamp. These pictures are from twenty-five years ago. These are pictures of your mother."

I gasped. My eyes expanded. I knew we looked alike, but this resemblance was uncanny. I mean, I really thought I was looking at myself. It was like I was her clone. I flipped through the pictures over and over again. In each one, my mother was getting a shot or drinking some liquid or getting examined by someone who looked a lot like a young Mr. Witherall, except with two real eyes.

"I think it's time you had a long talk with your mother. You have to find out why she knows Mr. Witherall. Maybe it has something to do with your powers."

I gathered all the papers from off the table and stuffed them back into the envelope.

"Where are you going? What are you going to do?" Tai asked as I headed toward the door.

"I'm going to show this to my parents. They have to tell me the truth." I put the envelope in my bicycle basket and started my ride home. I was so focused on trying to figure out what to say to my parents that I didn't notice a black van following me.

When it pulled up next to me, I got really nervous and pedaled faster. Then it got so close to me I almost swerved off the road in order avoid crashing into it. Suddenly, the side door of the van slid open and a hand reached out. As I was pulled inside, my bike went clattering to the side of the road. I tried to scream, but a rag was jammed into my mouth and a needle went into my arm. Seconds later, everything went black.

Chapter 14
Captured: Part II

So that's how I ended up tied to a chair. At first I thought maybe it was retaliation from Chester for that time I tied him to the chair and put him on the street corner. But then I remembered that Chester couldn't tie his own shoelaces, let alone the sophisticated knot that held my hands behind my back.

I wiggled and struggled against the ropes, but nothing happened. Ugh, I needed my super strength. Maybe if I wished hard enough, they'd come back. I closed my eyes and tried that. Nope, nothing.

"Good morning, Priscilla. Welcome back," an eerie voice said from … from everywhere. The deep sinister voice surrounded me as if it poured out of the walls. And it was Mr. Witherall's voice. He had kidnapped me!

I had to figure out a way to get out of here. If my life was going to play out like a comic book, now was the time for the great escape or the big rescue. Any second some spandex clad hero was going to drop in from the ceiling, take out the Goliath with a gun who was guarding me, and get me out of here. I stared up at the ceiling. Nothing. I guess it was up to me to come up with the brilliant plan. Fortunately, I had one.

"Hey, hey you," I said to the human truck. He cast his cold blue eyes on me, and I nearly fell off of the chair at how harsh and scary he looked.

"I gotta go to the bathroom," I said.

He looked away without responding. I knew a simple pretty please wasn't going to work.

"Seriously, it's an emergency. I really, really, really have to pee!"

Still no response.

"Look, either let me go to the bathroom or put me in a diaper 'cause something's coming out of me in about thirty seconds. Your choice."

He looked around as if waiting for a command.

"Let her use the facilities," Mr. Witherall's voice said.

After peeing for what felt like twenty minutes straight, I looked around the completely bare stainless steel bathroom. These people could really use the help of an interior designer. There wasn't even a mirror or a medicine cabinet where I could search for something flammable. Not that it would matter since I didn't have fire power. I paced the tiny room and tried to think about how my powers came the last time. I remembered Tai saying something about how they were probably tied to my hormones, especially since it happened near my time of the month. I also remembered that, at first, the hot flashes came every time I thought about Spencer. I tried thinking about Spencer. Nothing. Great. Now what would I do?

I sat on the toilet and put my head in my hands. The only other thing I remember from that day was Kyle knocking on the door to taunt me about some stupid game. Why was I thinking about Kyle again of all things? I still couldn't believe he liked me enough to put my name in his locker. That's just crazy. But, then again, he *was* pretty cute. And I loved all the competitions we had against each other. He was really able to keep me from getting bored when Tai was away. And he had really pretty lips. I bet they were really soft, too, and … wait a minute…that brought the heat. I definitely felt a hot flash coming.

I put the trash can on top of the sink right under the smoke alarm and filled it with toilet paper. After setting it on fire, I waited for the smoke to rise to the smoke detector while heating up the door knob. As soon as the alarm went off, the sprinkler system came on and a commotion erupted all over the building. I heard my personal guard approach the door. But when he turned the knob, he cried out in pain. I burst through the door, knocking him to the floor as he clutched his burnt hand.

Red and white lights flashed in the hallway as people in white lab coats were ushered out of the building by the armed men in bullet-proof vests. After rounding a corner, I tried to walk calmly yet quickly and not draw attention to myself, but a twelve-year-old redheaded girl in jean shorts didn't really blend in. Seconds later, someone yelled, "There she is. Get her!" I took off running even though I had no idea where I was going. I rounded another corner and ran headfirst into the rock-solid chest of an armed guard.

"I've got her," he said into an ear piece, grabbing my arm. I noticed eight or ten more guards running up behind him. "She's not going anywhere," he added, squeezing my arm tighter.

"That's what you think!" I touched his black pants and set them on fire. Then I kicked his legs out from under him and pushed his burning body into the guards behind him like I was playing a game of ten-pin bowling. I think I got a strike.

I ran past the flaming pile of pinheads and continued my escape.

Suddenly, a strong pair of arms wrapped around my waist. When I tried to scream, a hand went over my mouth. The strong arms pulled me into a dark room. I wiggled free and kicked my assailant in the shin.

"Ahh!" he cried in pain. I didn't care. I kicked him again then headed toward the door. "Priss, wait. It's me, Dad."

Chapter 15

Game Over?

"Daddy?" I turned on the light and took a good look at the man who had grabbed me. Even though he looked almost exactly like the other armed guards—bald, muscular, dressed in black, and carrying not one but three guns—I knew he was my daddy. I tackled him with a hug.

I didn't realize I was crying until my dad said, "Don't cry, Priss. We're gonna get you out of here."

I looked around the room. "Where are we? What is this place? What do they want with me?" I said, wiping my tears. From the desk, the ceiling-to-floor book shelf, and the leather sofa, it kind of looked like we were in a doctor's office. And I did remember seeing people in white lab coats running through the halls. But if this was some sort of hospital or medical building, why were there huge men with guns running around? And why did the huge men look so much like my father?

My dad leaned against a file cabinet and massaged his leg. "My God, Priss. I think you might have fractured my tibia."

"Your what?"

"Shinbone."

"I'm sorry, Daddy. I'm kinda strong. There's a lot about me you don't know."

"I figured as much." My dad limped to the corner of the room, aimed one of his guns at a shiny silver object hanging from the ceiling, and fired. It made a whining sound as pieces of it fell to the floor.

"What was that?"

"Surveillance camera. I don't want them to see what I plan to do next. We only have a few seconds before they start busting through that door. Barricade us in," he said, pointing to the door.

As I pushed the large filing cabinet in front of the door, I said, "You didn't answer the question, Dad. What is this place?"

"This is the Selliwood Institute in Colorado. I used to work here. When you didn't come home from school, I searched for you all over town. I finally found Tai and she told me about Witherall. I had no idea he was posing as your teacher. How could I have been so careless?" He closed his eyes and shook his head.

Careless? He thought he was careless? My dad was the most careful person I knew. I always thought he was just paranoid, but he was only trying to protect me. He obviously had good reason to be so worried about my safety.

"Anyway," he continued, "I knew he'd bring you here so I put on my old uniform, stole an access card, and snuck in. I've been blending in for the past hour while I searched for you. I'm pretty sure they know I'm here now, though."

"You knew I would be here? How? Why?"

He sighed. "Your mother and I met here. I was a guard, she was a ... patient."

"A patient? Was she sick?"

My father didn't answer immediately. He placed his ear against the wall opposite the door and started tapping it as if he were listening for something.

"Not exactly." He apparently found what he was looking for, as he stopped the tapping and started pressing buttons on one of his guns. It wasn't the same gun he used to shoot out the camera. It was more like a rectangle, about a foot long, and had ten black buttons in the shape of a triangle on one side of it. The only reason I knew it was some sort of gun was because it had a trigger on one end and a barrel on the other. It looked very high-tech, like something from *Star Trek*. "Priss, this might hurt a little, but it'll only be for a few seconds," he said, kneeling in front of me. "Cover your ears and try to put your mind somewhere else." Then he stood, aimed the gun at the wall, and fired.

The sound of that gun firing was so loud it felt like something inside my brain exploded. Time seemed to stand still as I felt the same painful sensation I had from Mr. Witherall's pen, except all over my body. Thankfully, it only lasted a second.

"What was that?" I exclaimed once it was over. My dad helped me to my feet. Apparently, I had collapsed to the floor and gotten into a fetal position.

"That was an Ion Distorter," he said, indicating the weird rectangular gun. "It was the quickest way for me to disintegrate the wall. I tried to find a place that was hollow so I wouldn't have to use it for long. It's painful for you, but won't cause any permanent damage."

"Painful for me? Just me? Why not you?" I asked as I followed him into the hole in the wall he had just created.

We entered a narrow tunnel that was barely big enough for him to fit in. He had to turn sideways in order to walk.

"You and your mother have a few different ions in the atoms that make up your cells than Josh and me. We're not sure about the twins because they're not old enough. They could still develop the mutation at puberty."

"Excuse me, what?"

He sighed. "If we hurry, we can make it to the warehouse and out of the building in seventy-three seconds. I'll try to explain in that amount of time." Without slowing his step, he began the story. "Your mother was a genetic experiment created right here in this building. The Selliwood Institute began in 1968 in the midst of the

Vietnam War as a training facility for volunteer members of the military in order to create an elite team of special operatives. But they quickly found that too many of them were killed or injured in battle, thus losing their monetary investment. That's when Colonel Selliwood teamed up with Dr. Witherall, a brilliant geneticist. Together, they used science to give their soldiers genetic advantages. They wanted to create an indestructible human. But most of the time, the soldiers' bodies would reject the mutation or cause … disturbing side effects. They decided to start the genetic mutations earlier so they would be accepted in the body. After sixteen unsuccessful attempts, they succeeded with the birth of your mother. By the time she was your age, she could vanquish a hundred men in a matter of minutes without even breaking a sweat."

"So, my mother is a murderer?"

My father looked at me. I could tell from the sad expression in his blue eyes that he wanted to hug me, but he didn't have time. "No, Priss. That's what they wanted her to be, but she rebelled. The summer before I went to college, I came to work here. We fell in love, and I helped her escape. Twenty years ago, we used this very same secret tunnel to get away. I just hope it works a second time."

I noticed a bit of doubt and worry in his voice. I had to admit, I was worried too. What were the chances that they hadn't discovered this secret passage after almost twenty years?

After what was probably seventy-three seconds exactly, we entered a large room. It was pitch black but I could sense the size of it. Unfortunately, I could also hear people breathing. I feared there were at least thirty people in the room. When the lights clicked on, my fears were confirmed.

We stared directly into the locked and loaded barrels of more than two dozen rifles, pistols, and machine guns. I felt like I was in a video game, only I couldn't hit pause or use a cheat to get to the next level. This was real. And soon it would be game over for me and Dad.

"Really, Gregory? The same tunnel?" Mr. Witherall said, emerging from behind a wall of guards. "Lack of imagination has always been your downfall. Did you really think I'd let you slip away with another one of my creations?"

"She's not your creation. She's my daughter."

"A minor detail that I won't fault her for. I'm quite impressed with her abilities so far. Who would have thought that a second-generation specimen would be so extraordinary? Thank goodness for that local news program she appeared on. Imagine my surprise when we got a hit on our face recognition technology from River's Butt, Pennsylvania. At first I thought it had to be her mother. But I'm even more pleased at meeting Priscilla. I can't wait to study her."

Mr. Witherall smiled and reached toward me, but my dad stepped in front of him and said, "You won't touch her." My father engaged his rifle and pointed it at Mr. Witherall, causing all of the guards to point their guns at my father.

Mr. Witherall rolled his eyes, or shall I say eye. "Like you have any say in the matter. Just give up, Gregory. It's over."

Suddenly, the air in the warehouse stirred. It kinda felt like a tornado was coming, except we were indoors. The lights flickered on and off. When they stopped, my mother stood between my father and Mr. Witherall and said, "Let my family go and I might let you live."

Chapter 16

She's Like the Wind

In unison, the guns shifted from my father to my mother. She didn't flinch. She didn't even acknowledge their existence. To her, there was no one else in the room besides Mr. Witherall. Her red hair cascaded over her shoulders and down her back. It seemed to wave back and forth in a non-existent breeze. Her white spandex catsuit hugged every curve of her body. And, wow, was she curvy. I had never seen my mother dressed in so little. Like my father, she always wore business suits, usually a size too large. She tried to hide her amazing figure. Now I knew why. She didn't want to have to explain why she was an almost forty-year-old mother of four with the body of a superhero.

Mr. Witherall waved his hand in the air, and immediately, all the guards lowered their weapons. "Specimen Q. It's about time you showed up. I was afraid you wouldn't be joining us."

"This has gone far enough. It's me you want. Let them go."

"Specimen Q—"

"My name is Quindolyn."

Mr. Witherall smiled at my mother. But it wasn't a friendly smile. It was the kind of smile that an adult gives a child when the child says they want to be called Cinderella or Batman instead of their given name.

"Quindolyn," he began again.

"How's that eye of yours?" My mother interjected with a smirk.

Mr. Witherall touched his eye self-consciously.

"I'd be happy to give you a matching set," she added.

He clenched his jaw. So it was my mother who had damaged his eye. I felt a surge of pride—something I had never felt toward her before.

"Look, Quindolyn, I forgive you for everything. If it were up to me, you and your so-called family could walk out of here right now. But it's not up to me. Colonel Selliwood actually wants you and your daughter dead. You and Priscilla are a dangerous liability. And you've cost him millions of dollars over the past four years, stealing his specimens."

"We're not specimens. We're human beings and we deserve a normal life."

"I don't want to argue with you, Quindolyn. I want to help you. I'll convince Selliwood not to kill you, if you let me study Priscilla. We need to learn everything she's capable of. What if her genetic mutations are causing side effects? She may need medication. I can help her." Mr. Witherall tried to sound comforting and reassuring, but I wasn't fooled. His raspy voice still gave me the creeps.

"You're not drugging my child like you did to me for seventeen years." My mother's cheeks turned red. The memories of her childhood must have really angered her. I couldn't imagine her pain. "I'm going to say this one time. Let my family go or die a horribly painful death. The choice is yours."

I didn't know how this stand-off was going to end. Someone had to make a move. I was so distracted by the icy conversation between my mother and Mr. Witherall, I didn't notice that the bad guys had already made a move.

"You chose wrong," my mother said, shaking her head. Apparently, she was more aware of her surroundings than I was. She yelled, "Priss, down!" as she turned and grabbed a small metal object out of her belt. I hit the floor as fast as I could as the metal object flew over my head and into the knee of a guard who had snuck up behind me. Gun fire exploded from all directions. "Greg, rafters!"

"I'm on it," my father responded, firing a gun at the guards in the upper levels.

Mr. Witherall retreated into the depths of the warehouse. Five or six huge guards leaped toward my mother, and she fended each of them off like an Amazon warrior with a black belt. I could barely keep up with her arms, legs, and feet moving in every direction, causing ridiculous amounts of pain to the truck-sized guards. At one point she picked up a guard and swung him like a bat, knocking out several others. She moved so quickly around the room, disarming and disabling the guards, that it was almost like watching the wind.

"Priss, hide!" my father said as he jammed the butt of his gun into another man's stomach. I didn't want to hide. I wanted to help, but I didn't know how. I didn't want to get in the way.

"Greg, get Dr. Witherall," my mother called over the noise of combat.

My dad looked around and found Witherall making a break for the exit. He tried to follow, but his leg put him at a huge disadvantage. Witherall got away.

Once carefully hidden behind some barrels, I noticed a guard about twenty feet away from me not involved in the fighting. He was pushing buttons on the side of a silver rectangular gun. It was an Ion Distorter. I couldn't let him fire it. My mother wouldn't be able to defend herself if she felt anything close to the amount of pain it caused me.

I had to stop him, but I couldn't come from behind the barrels. With all the bullets flying everywhere, I could easily get hit. I stared at my hands. I wondered if I could gather enough strength to shoot fire twenty feet. I didn't have too much time to wonder. The guard steadied the gun and prepared to shoot. I felt the hot flash rise within me, and with all my might, I thrust it forward. A stream of fire sliced through the air. Just as he pulled back on the trigger, the fire reached the tip of the gun and melted it. The lights on the side of it stopped flashing. I did it! I stared at my hands in amazement.

More guards entered the warehouse from all directions. Even though my parents dominated every person that came at them, I didn't know how they would be able to keep up at their frantic pace. How were we going to get out?

Priss, can you hear me? a voice inside my head said. And this time it really was inside my head.

"Mom, is that you?" I asked, looking over to where my mother's foot had connected with one man's head while a swift swipe from her hand broke another man's arm at the elbow. I was pretty sure her lips weren't moving—although she was moving so fast I couldn't be positive. How could she possibly be talking to me? "How can I hear you?" I felt ridiculous talking out loud with all the commotion going on, but I really wanted to know.

I'll explain later. Right now, your dad and I need your help. The barrels to your left under the white sheets contain nitromethane. It's highly flammable. I need you to set them on fire then run for the exit.

"What about you and Dad?"

We'll be right behind you. I promise.

My heartbeat tripled its pace. What if I blew up the barrels and Mom and Dad didn't make it out in time? What if I killed my own parents? No, I couldn't do it. I started shaking my head in a frantic protest as tears swelled behind my eyes. But then that calmness returned. Suddenly, I understood where the feeling came from. It was my mother. She was somehow soothing my anxiety. I guess it had something to do with the way she was able to speak to me telepathically. She was also able to show me what I needed to do and how to do it.

I realized that my mother had always been with me. I was so unfair to her. Part of me had hated her for being away so much. But it wasn't her fault. She had important work to do, protecting other children from being victims of horrible scientific experiments. Even though she was away physically, she did her best to be with me ... telepathically, I guess.

As if on auto-pilot, I whipped off the three sheets over the barrels and tied them together, making a long rope.

I paused and watched my parents fighting for their lives, for our lives. It was my fault we were in this position. I should have trusted my dad more and avoided publicity.

Priss, now! my mother yelled in my head. Without further hesitation, I lit my makeshift fuse then ran as fast as I could out the doors of the warehouse, praying that my parents would make it out as well.

Chapter 17

The Most Awesome Thing in the World

I ran outside, where the morning sun peeked out behind mountains. Once a safe distance away, I turned and saw the building light up. A split second after I heard the explosion, I felt the bits of metal, wood, and other stuff flying around me. A loud boom rattled my ears. I fell to my knees and covered my head with my hands. *Oh my God. They didn't get out.* I couldn't breathe. I felt like my heart had turned to stone and crushed the air out of my lungs.

I had to go back and get them. I couldn't let it end like this. Not after all they'd done for me. I'd been such an insensitive and selfish brat. I couldn't believe the way

I'd spoken to my mother, actually accusing her of not loving me. And she had gone and given her life to save me.

No. No. No. I wasn't going to let this happen. I needed my parents. I needed my father to walk me down the aisle one day. I needed my mother to teach me how to deal with my abilities. Josh and the twins would be devastated, and it would be my fault. How would I ever be able to look at them and explain that I let our parents die?

I wiped away the tears and stood, preparing myself to go back in there and drag my parents out. I knew my body could stand the heat, and even if it couldn't, I would rather share their fate than live on without them.

I ran toward the building just as another series of explosions rippled through it. I fell to the ground again and hugged my knees. I rocked back and forth, letting the tears flow. Who was I kidding? There was no way they survived those blasts.

"I love you, Mommy," I said, although a painful knot in my throat made it difficult to speak. "I'll always love you."

I love you too, Priss, my mother's voice said. She must have been communicating with me from the afterlife.

"Mommy, I'm so sorry. Can you ever forgive me?"

For what?

"For killing you."

Killing me? Priss, I'm not dead. I'm right behind you.

Eyes still filled with tears, I turned around and had to do a double-take. My dad lay motionless on the ground. My mother knelt over him, running her fingers over his smooth bald head.

"What ... how ... when did ..." I stammered, looking back and forth between the burning building and my parents not ten feet away.

"I'm really fast," my mother said, winking at me.

"But I didn't see ... how did ..." The answers to the gazillion questions in my mind really didn't matter. My parents were alive. That was the important thing. I ran and wrapped my arms around my mother. Even though she was covered in ash and smelled like burnt hair, I buried my face into her shoulder. "What's wrong with Dad?" I asked when I noticed he hadn't moved.

"I run faster than the speed of sound. Too fast for normal humans. He passed out from the force, but he should be fine in a few minutes."

Seconds later, he groaned. His eyes fluttered open. "You did the running thing again, didn't you?" he asked, staring into my mother's eyes with so much love I kind of felt like I was interrupting a special moment.

My mother smiled at him. "I had to get us out." Then she leaned down and kissed him. Usually, old people kissing really grossed me out. Every time my mother came home from one of her "business trips," my parents were all over each other so much that once I had to down a bottle of Pepto-Bismol to keep from puking. I always thought they were way too excited to see each other. But now I understood that each time my mother went away, Dad feared for her life. He never knew whether she would make it back or not. And even though she had super powers, she was still human ... mostly.

"I'm gonna have a headache for a week." My father leaned up on his elbows, and my mother and I helped him to his feet.

"So, how do we get out of here?" I asked, taking a good look around for the first time. We were completely surrounded by mountains that seemed to hug a soft blue sky. It would have been the perfect vacation spot if crazy men in lab coats weren't trying to cut me open and study me a few feet away.

"Fly," my mother said simply as if it were completely obvious. She buried her face into my father's chest as he stroked her head and kissed her hair. Okay, the public displays of affection were starting to get out of hand.

I turned my back to them and tried to figure out what she meant by flying. Once again, I was confused. Could she fly? Maybe my dad and I were going to ride on her back as she flew us home. Or maybe *I* could fly. I'd never tried. Maybe that was another one of my powers. I spread my arms out and tried to jump as high as I could. Nothing. I tried flapping my arms like a bird. Once again, nothing. I did this several times until I heard snickering behind me.

"What are you doing?" my mother asked.

"You said we were flying home, so I'm trying to fly." I turned around and saw that my father was laughing so hard he clutched his side.

"No, honey. We're taking the jet," she said, smiling.

I looked and looked, even turning around several times. I didn't see any jet.

"Oh, right," my mother added while pressing buttons on her silver belt.

I heard a *whoosh* sound, and then right before my eyes, a black jet appeared. It looked like one of those jets from those awesome air shows. I didn't know exactly where in the world we were, but I knew we would be able to get home within minutes using that thing.

"So, what else can you do, Mom?" I asked once we were in the jet. It was more spacious than it looked from the outside, kinda like a winged Mercedes with four plush tan leather seats in the cockpit and sixteen more seats in the back.

There were a lot less controls and buttons than I expected. In front of the pilot and copilot seats, there was a W-shaped wheel with buttons on it, kind of like a Playstation game controller. I couldn't wait to get my hands on it. Oh, that would be the ultimate racing game. Well, I guess it would be a flying game. In any case, I knew I could master it in seconds.

"Well, besides speed, telepathy, and super hearing, I'm pretty strong, but apparently not as strong as you. I really think you broke your father's leg." She helped my father into one of the back seats and rested his leg on the seat next to it.

"Sorry, Dad," I said again. I really did feel guilty.

"No, prob, Priss. Your mom has done worse to me. Remember that time you put me in a coma for two weeks, Quin?"

"Must you always bring that up?" My mother rolled her eyes and started walking toward the cockpit.

"What happened?" I asked, curious about my parents' mysterious life.

"Your mother tried to use her telepathy on me and nearly killed me," he said with a smile. I think he enjoyed teasing her.

"It was a long time ago. I didn't know how to control it. I was just trying to tell you I liked you." My mother winked at my father then entered the cockpit. She sat in the pilot's seat and clicked several buttons on the jet game controller, and the plane lifted straight in the air a few feet and started to hum.

"What else? What else?" I hurried and buckled into the copilot's chair. I was so excited. I wanted to know everything.

My mother pressed a few more buttons; we went higher into the air and then took off as if we just got shot out of a slingshot. It was the most awesome thing in the world.

"Well, I have a bit of telekinesis," she said after a few moments.

"What's that?"

"I can move things with my mind."

"Seriously? That is so awesome. What about all those moves you were using in the warehouse? Is that part of your powers, too?"

"No, that's part of years of training. I've been trained in boxing, kickboxing, karate, fencing, taekwondo, and judo since the day I started walking. It's not the life I wanted for myself. I didn't want to exist only to kill people. I wanted to create life. I wanted to have children, a husband, and a house with a white picket fence in the suburbs."

My mother sighed and looked down at her hands on the steering wheel. It was hard for me to imagine what her life was like. I admired her for having the strength to choose her own path. It must have been so hard for her to leave everything she knew and run off with my father. Maybe that's why she never showed emotion before. Maybe she felt she had to hold it all in to give my brothers and me the safest, happiest life possible. But I was a little confused about something.

"But, Mom, if you finally got everything you wanted with Dad, why are you never home with us?"

She sighed again and glanced back at my father, who had fallen asleep in one of the backseats. "I *did* have everything I wanted, but my happiness was stymied by a tugging at my soul. I felt the cries for help from my brothers and sisters who were still held prisoner at Selliwood. So I worked on strengthening my psychic abilities and forming connections with those who wanted to escape. Four years ago, I started working full-time at getting them out. Each rescue takes months of planning and telepathic communication. Once I help someone escape, I move them to another part of the world and stay with them until they adjust to life on the outside."

"So you keep breaking into the Selliwood Institute? Do you have to fight your way out like that every time?"

"It usually doesn't get that physical, but, yes, I do often have to use my martial arts training. In between rescues, I also intercept as many assassination attempts ordered by the institute as I can. Those are usually guaranteed to turn into hand-to-hand combat. You should probably learn some moves yourself for self-defense. With your natural gymnastics ability, it should come pretty easy to you. I can teach you if you like."

"Really?" I nearly jumped out of my seat. Thankfully, I was buckled up. "That would be awesome."

"Then again, maybe I shouldn't." She turned her green eyes to me and bit her lip in thought. "These powers that I have … that *we* have, they're not to be taken lightly. I'll train you if you want, but you have to promise you won't use your abilities on frivolities. I don't want to hear about you eavesdropping on private conversations or getting revenge by damaging personal property."

I sunk down into my seat guiltily. Those were things I had already done.

"Yes, ma'am."

"As a matter of fact, no one can know about this. I've managed to rescue six people from the Selliwood Institute. Three have already been recaptured. Four months ago, I completely lost psychic connection with the children. Something's wrong. I can't figure out what Selliwood is planning next."

"But didn't I just blow up the institute? Shouldn't it be all over now?"

My mother shook her head and then turned her attention back toward the sky. "I wish it were that easy, Priss. That was just a section of the institute. A minor section at that. It will be rebuilt with different access codes and tighter security. What we need to do is get into the central control room and destroy that place from the inside out. But I can't do that with so many innocent children inside."

Suddenly my mind flooded with images of some scary looking building.

"Whoa, wait, what is going on in my head right now?" I asked trying to shake the images away.

"Oh, sorry Priss. I must have inadvertently teleported my memories of the Institute. I'll retreat from your mind now."

"No, it's okay. Just a little warning would be nice."

My mother took a deep breath and then sent me some much more calmer mental images of the Institute. She showed me what looked like a blue print of the entire facility and then zoomed in on what I assumed was the central control room. She even showed me the sequence of buttons I needed to press to activate the self destruct sequence.

"So, Mom, why did Mister ... or Doctor ... or whatever he is Witherall keep calling you Specimen Q?" I asked when I finished my virtual tour of the Selliwood Institute.

"Specimen Q is my given name. The seventeenth letter of the English alphabet. Before me, there were sixteen failed attempts. After me, they finished using the letters of the English alphabet and then started naming the specimens after the Greek alphabet."

"So how many more are out there?"

"Thirty." My mother clenched her jaw. Saying that number clearly upset her. I searched my mind for a reason, and after a little simple math, I think I figured it out.

"Shouldn't there be a few more than that?"

"Specimen Y died in combat." She took a deep breath and added, "Specimen Beta was killed while trying to escape."

I didn't want to ask any more questions. I had a feeling Beta was a friend of hers. Maybe she had even watched Beta die. I shook off the thought. It was too much to bear. I don't know what I'd do if something happened to one of my friends. If Kyle or Tai were killed because of me, I'd never be able to forgive myself.

Instead of talking, I watched as my mother effortlessly maneuvered the super cool jet and tried not to think of the pain that so-called institute had caused so many people.

As if she read my mind, my mother said, "You want to try it?" while nodding toward the control. Well, now that I think about it, she probably *did* read my mind.

Too excited to actually speak a syllable, I just bounced in my seat like a puppy about to get a treat. My mother pressed a button and immediately the jet started spiraling down. "She's all yours," she said, pointing to the copilot's steering wheel and unbuckling her seatbelt.

"Where are you going? What do I do?" I yelled above the sound of the wind rushing against the jet.

"Press that button there and that button there and then pull up and keep us level. I'm going to go visit with your father."

"But, Mom, I don't know what I'm doing!"

"You'll figure it out."

Moments later, after I managed to keep the jet from crashing, I relaxed a little and heard my parents whispering.

"So you mean to tell me you knew about Priss' powers the whole time?" my dad said. "Why didn't you tell me?"

"I wanted to tell you in person. I didn't want you to panic and do something overprotective and crazy."

"You can't keep secrets like that from me, Quin. She's my child, too."

"Well, speaking of secrets, I think we need to talk about—" My mother stopped abruptly. "Hold on. She's listening."

Then everything went silent.

Chapter 18

The Hottest Girl in River's Bend

After landing the jet in an isolated section of woods, we piled in to the family car and made the short drive back to River's Bend. On the way, we stopped at the hospital, where they took care of my dad's leg. Yep, it was broken.

My parents wanted to keep all that had happened secret from Josh, but I wouldn't let them. I knew he needed to know. All these lies weren't healthy. Besides, I thought this new information would get his mind off of what Stefanie had done to him.

So, as a family, we sat around the kitchen table while Mom and Dad explained their past and what we had just been through over the past twenty-four hours. When they were finished, Josh didn't say a word. He looked back and forth between my parents and me. Then he chewed his thumbnail.

"Are you okay, honey?" My mother reached out to touch his shoulder, but he jerked away. Then he stood up, looked at all of us again, and sulked off to his room.

"Joshua, you get back here!" My father tried to run after him but hadn't quite mastered movement with his new cast. He ended up falling back into his chair with a thud.

"Let him go," my mother said with a worried expression on her face. I got the feeling there was something going on with Josh that she knew about and wasn't sharing.

I couldn't think about Josh for too long because the twins started bombarding me with stupid questions.

"Can you really start a fire with your fingers?"

"Can you melt things?"

"Can we roast marshmallows with your fingers?"

"Oh, s'mores! Let's make s'mores with your hands, Priss!"

"We are not going to use my powers to make snack food," I snapped. Charlie and Chester both poked out their bottom lips in a disappointed pout. I sighed and looked at my mother, asking permission. She shrugged. I guess she was okay with it as long as no one saw. "Oh, what the hay?" I said. The next thing I knew, I was in the backyard frying s'mores from ten feet away, much to the delight of my little brothers.

An hour later, Josh still hadn't come out of his room, and my parents had retreated to the basement. I tried to use my super hearing to figure out what they were saying, but my mother was apparently able to block me like she had when we were on the jet. All I knew was that they were talking about Josh.

Even though the twins had eaten enough chocolate and marshmallows to explode, I still couldn't convince them to call it a night and head inside. They kept wanting me to light things on fire. After melting the heads of half of their G.I. Joe dolls … I mean "action figures," I was finally rescued by the door bell.

"I'll get it!" I yelled, even though Josh and my parents were still MIA so I was the only one able to get it anyway. "Hey, Kyle. What are you doing here?" I asked when I opened the door.

Kyle stared at the ground and ran his fingers through his freshly cut hair. It looked more blond than usual. He probably had to get it dyed for a photo shoot or something. It really suited him, though. I hated to admit it, but he looked pretty gorgeous in his khakis and blue sweater vest that matched his eyes perfectly. "Uh, I called, but no one answered," he said.

That made sense. My parents had unplugged the phone when they started to explain everything to us. But I didn't really understand why he was calling me. So I kinda just stared at him, waiting for him to say something else.

"Um, I got these for you," he said, pulling what looked like a bouquet of candy from behind his back. "They're raspberry crème lollipops from Willie's. I know they're your favorite." As I looked at the arrangement of lollipops tied together with a red ribbon, it finally hit me why he was there. I totally forgot I agreed to play *Street Mania* with him that night. It was kinda like a date and I kinda stood him up. I felt terrible.

"Do you want to come in and play video games?"

He nodded, but didn't take a step toward the door.

"Uh, Kyle, it's gonna be kinda hard for you to play from the front porch. The controller cord won't reach."

Kyle gave a nervous laugh and stared down at the ground. "I kinda don't wanna play."

"Why? Afraid I'll beat you again?" I punched him in the arm as lightly as I could. I didn't want to break anyone else's bones tonight.

"I kinda just wanted to ask you something." His voice jumped up an octave on the word *something*. It was really, really cute. I felt a little tingle in my stomach.

"What?"

"Do you ... dance ... River ... do ... go." He stopped, took a deep breath, and blurted, "Do you want to go to the River Day Dance with me?"

My eyes nearly popped out of my skull. Kyle Montgomery asked me, Priscilla Sumner, to the River Day Dance. This was huge. Yes, it was a stupid little tradition with lame costumes and square dancing, but it was also a very sentimental occasion. Town tradition stated that if you married your first date to the River Day Dance, you were guaranteed to live happily ever after.

"I know you think I'm a jerk and I'm probably not your type," he added when I didn't respond immediately. "But I can't stop thinking about you. You're super cool, super cute, and you're the only girl I know who can kick my butt at anything. You're the hottest girl I know."

Hot? He thought I was hot? He had no idea.

Part Two

Chapter 19

Josh, the Prophet

It started with a fever. But to a girl who can shoot fire out of her fingers, a fever is no big deal. Unfortunately, things got much worse.

It was Wednesday and Kyle had walked me home from school. As soon as I said good-bye to him on my front porch, the lightheadedness started. I had a hard time holding my head up straight. I lay down on the couch for a minute, but every time I tried to sit up, my head would flop forward or backward. Then my balance went all haywire. I'm not saying I've ever been super graceful or anything, but I thought I had mastered walking through the living room without falling on my face when I was like three.

Mom and Dad sent me to my room and fussed over me like I was dying.

"I knew it," my dad said, pacing my room with his crutches while Mom stuck a needle in my arm. "They probably poisoned her or something while she was in that place. We need to get her to a doctor and get her a full physical."

"You know we can't do that, Greg. Even a first-year med student would see her blood isn't normal," Mom said, looking at the tube of blood she'd just collected. I wondered if she could see the little microscopic mutations in me with her naked eye. Then she levitated the tube to my father. "Run some tests on it, honey. Put that Biochemistry degree you have to good use. If something's really wrong—"

"If something's really wrong, we are out of here, Quin. I mean it. New house, new state, new names, everything. I can't believe I let you talk me into staying here in the first place. What if they come back for her?"

Dad's face turned red. He was really angry about this. I had no idea he'd wanted to move away and Mom talked him out of it. Whatever she'd said to him, I'm glad it worked. I didn't want to leave River's Bend. I couldn't leave my best friends.

Mom and Dad stared at each other in a silent stalemate. I felt I needed to lighten the mood.

"Britney!" I yelled.

"What?" they said in unison, turning their attention to me.

"Yeah, Britney. If Dad is handing out new names, I wanna be Britney. It's about time someone brought some honor back to that name after what the Spears girl did to it."

My mother actually grinned at my little joke. My dad rolled his eyes and headed for the door.

* * *

Josh was still acting weird. He locked himself in his room for three days, even missing school and football practice. The only clue I had he was even still alive was that every few hours his soundtrack of depressing white boy music changed. If I had to listen to one more Elliott Smith album, I was going to scream.

After a couple of hours of lying in my bed, I heard a light tapping on the door. Josh entered the room quietly. He stepped in and closed the door behind him, the whole time not making eye contact with me.

"Are you feeling better?" he asked, still not looking at me. He crossed his arms and stared out of my window.

"I'm fine, Josh. It's just a bug or something. It'll pass." I felt weird reassuring him that I was fine. He normally didn't worry about my health. We left the worrying to Dad; he was paranoid enough for all of us.

I rolled over on the bed and stared at my brother more closely. He looked really small and really pale, and I thought I saw his lip trembling, like he was going to cry or something. *What the heck is the matter with him?* "Josh, are you okay?"

"I've known you all your life. I was there the day you were born. Twelve years. In twelve years, you've never had so much as a cold."

I opened my mouth to protest, but then I thought about it. He was right. I had never been sick, ever. Then suddenly I come home from school and I can't walk straight. It was kind of weird. "Well, that's no big deal. I mean, there's a first time for everything, right?"

Josh sat on my window seat and put his head in his hands.

"Okay, you're really scaring me, Josh. What's going on?" I asked, leaning up on one elbow. I was too weak to sit all the way up.

He sighed and looked at me before saying, "The thing is, I can see things."

I rolled my eyes and flopped back on the bed. "Well, you have eyes. I should hope you can see things."

"Don't be a pain, Priss. I'm serious here." Josh jumped up and kicked a basketball and a baseball glove that littered the floor of my messy room.

"Okay, fine. What can you see?" I said, trying to hide my sarcasm.

"The future."

Two months ago I would have busted out laughing at something so ridiculous. But that was before I started shooting fire out of my fingers. For all I knew, he could really see the future. That wouldn't be the strangest ability of a Sumner. I mean, my mother had gotten in the habit of using her telekinesis to cook dinner. It was pretty freaky to walk in the kitchen and see salt levitating in midair over a pot while my mother sat at the breakfast table flipping through a *Modern Science* magazine.

So instead of calling him crazy or something, I just said, "How do you know?"

"At first it was just little things," he said, sitting back down at the window seat and staring at his untied Chuck Taylors. "I would be able to predict what Dad was making for dinner or that the twins would break a lamp in the living room."

"Anyone could predict that."

"But then things started getting bigger. Like I had a vision that Stefanie would cheat on me, and she did."

I wanted to say that Stefanie was a skank and anyone could have predicted that as well, but I didn't want to hurt his feelings. I knew he still kinda loved her.

"I also had a vision that you and mom weren't exactly human, and that turned out to be true too."

I rested my head on the pillow and thought about this for a second. I guess Josh did have super powers like me and mom. But I didn't understand why he was so upset about it.

Looking at him, I said, "Well, so what? You can see the future. You should be happy. It's more useful than shooting fire out of your fingers. Go buy yourself a lottery ticket and stop complaining."

Josh rolled his eyes. "I knew I couldn't talk to you about this." He stood and headed toward the door.

"I'm sorry. I'm sorry. No more sarcasm. Promise." I held up my hands in surrender and waited for him to sit down again before saying, "But seriously, if you knew Stefanie was going to cheat on you, why were you so determined to give her a promise ring?"

"I tried to change the future. I tried to make it not come true."

"Why?"

Josh shut his eyes tightly. After taking a deep breath, he said, "Because if everything I see comes true, it means you're going to die."

Chapter 20
Sick of Love

"Die? I'm gonna die? Like dead die? Like game over, no extra player, no reset button?"

Josh nodded.

"Whoa." I couldn't think of anything else to say. We sat in silence for a few minutes while I let the information sink in. I wanted to believe Josh was wrong and that somehow he had made a mistake. But looking at him, I knew he was sure even though he didn't want to be. By the expression on his face, I knew it hurt him to have to tell me this.

"Do you know when? Do you know how? Maybe we can stop it from happening."

He sighed. "Yeah. I know how. You—"

Josh was interrupted by a knock on the door.

"Priss, it's me," came my mother's voice.

He gave me a panicked look. I knew he didn't want me to tell mom about his ability to see the future. He wasn't ready. I went through the same thing when I discovered my powers. It takes some getting used to. Plus, he probably didn't want to bring up the whole "me dying" thing. Mom might be able to handle it. She would sit down and try to think of a logical way to overcome it. Dad, on the other hand, would go into super-overprotective mode. He would probably take me to the hospital and force every vaccine known to man on me. Then he'd stand outside my door with a gun, day and night, ready to take out any possible threat to my life.

"Priss, can I come in?" What a refreshing question considering Dad often busted down my door if I didn't open it fast enough. He was always afraid I was in some sort of danger. I guess, in a way, he was right.

After a quick glance at Josh to make sure he was ready, I said, "Come in, Mom." I could tell Josh was trying to calm his nerves and clear his head. I tried to do the same although I probably wasn't as good at it as Josh.

I had to remember to ask him how he kept mom from reading his thoughts all the time.

My mom opened the door and stepped inside. Two pitchers of water hovered in front of her, held in place by her telekinesis. Totally creepy, yet kinda cool.

"Can I talk to your sister for a moment?" she asked Josh. He nodded and then bolted out of the room as if afraid his presence alone would reveal his secret.

"Okay, what's his name?" my mom asked once Josh was gone.

"Whose name?"

"The boy."

"What boy? Josh? Your son, Josh?"

"No, not Josh. I know my own child's name. I mean *the* boy. Your boyfriend."

"Boyfriend? He's not my—" Just then, a heat rose in me and swirled through my body. Before I could think to stop it, flames shot out of my fingers, setting my sheets on fire. I jumped out of bed and clasped my hands together. Flames spread across my bed, eating my favorite Wonder Woman sheets. Snap! Just when I thought I was getting the hang of this "finger shooting fire" thing, I go and set my bedroom on fire. I really wished these powers came with a guide book.

My mother calmly took one of the floating pitchers and poured it over the flames. Out of immediate danger, I fell to my knees and then lay down on the floor, too weak and tired to keep standing. I suddenly had the urge to vomit.

"Just as I thought. Priss, you're not sick. You're in love."

"Excuse me? I'm in love?"

"Love is a very strong emotion and it affects each person differently. For people like us, it can be downright dangerous."

"Well, if this is what love does to me, you better bring a coffin to my wedding."

"When I fell in love with your father," my mother continued, ignoring my sarcasm, "I put him in a coma for two weeks. And that was even though I'd had a lifetime of training with my powers. You've only known about your abilities for a little over a month. If you're not careful, you could kill him."

"Kill him?"

My mother picked up a t-shirt off the floor, sniffed it, convulsed a little, and then tossed it in my dirty clothes hamper. "Look at what you did to your bed just thinking about him. Can you imagine what would happen if you kissed him? And don't even think about sex. You have to pass a written test before you're ready for reproduction activity."

"Whoa, wait, what? A test?"

"Yes, to make sure you understand your body well enough. I created an educational video about hormone progression and its interaction with our specific genetic mutation. After you watch it, I want you to take a test to make sure you understand the implications."

I stared at her in disbelief. I didn't even want to imagine what this video was like. It was probably more embarrassing than the video they made us watch in sixth grade after separating the boys and the girls. The one with the corny folk music and the images of flowers blooming.

"There's no way I'm watching that video." I rolled over on the floor, turning my back to her.

"Sorry, Priss, you have to. For people with our genetic mutation, it's an absolute necessity that we understand our bodies."

"This is so unfair, so freaking unfair. What about Josh? He didn't have to watch it."

"Josh doesn't have powers." My mother went back to sniffing my floor clothes.

Hmph. That's what you think.

"What did you say?"

Having a telepathic mother really sucks. There's no such thing as private thoughts.

"Mom! I didn't *say* anything. I thought it. That's so unfair, Mom. You can't go reading my mind all the time. A girl needs privacy."

"I'm sorry, I'm sorry. You're right. I should stop that." She sat down at my window seat, continuing to clean my room with her telekinesis. I could feel her retreating from my mind, but I still didn't want what I knew about Josh to slip. I had to figure out some way to get her out of my head. So, I did the only thing I could think of. I set my curtains on fire.

"Whoa, Priscilla, you've really got it bad for this boy, don't you?" she said, emptying the other pitcher on my curtains. "I better go upload the video onto the family computer."

"Oh no, Mom. Not gonna happen. I don't need a sex video. I have no interest in having sex, and since I only have my powers for one week a month, I think I can avoid the whole boy-killing thing. I just won't go near him during that time."

"One week a month? Who said you only have your powers one week a month?"

I gathered my strength and sat up to look her directly in the eye. "I just assumed the only time I can shoot fire is when I'm ... you know, hormonal or something, like when I'm on or near my period."

My mother laughed so hard I thought I saw tears form in her eyes. "Priss, you're adorable." She shook her head and sighed, trying to get control over herself. "Honey, you have your powers all the time. They're a part of you." She stood up and headed for the door. "You have so much to learn.

"On your period," she said to herself before another fit of laughter.

Chapter 21

Freaks Like Us

My mom gave me some meditation techniques to control my "love episodes" as she so annoyingly nicknamed them. She said there was a drug she could inject in me to neutralize my hormones, but she wanted to leave that only for an emergency situation. After being medicated for so much of her life, she didn't want me to go through the same. She said I would have to learn to deal with the changes in my body naturally.

Once I got myself together, I had to go see Tai. I'd already told her about everything that happened at Selliwood. I knew it should have been a family secret or something, but Tai *was* family to me. There was no way I could keep it from her.

"You will not believe what my mother just told me," I said, bursting into her bedroom.

"What?" She closed her thick, brown, boring book and whipped off her glasses.

"She said if I don't learn to control my powers I could kill Kyle!"

"Holy hot dogs!"

"Yeah, fry him like a French fry." I flopped onto her perfectly neat bed with the sunflower sheets. Gosh, why was her room always so clean?

"Well that'll be pretty inconvenient when he tries to kiss you at the River Day Dance on Saturday."

"Whoa, wait, what?" I said, sitting up.

"It's all over school. Kyle plans on kissing you after the River Day Dance."

"All over school? Kissing?"

"I think it's kind of sweet. I mean, yes, it's a little weird that you and Kyle ... like each other or whatever. But when you think about, it's really sweet. You two have known each other your whole lives."

"Wait a minute. Let's back up a little. Kissing? Why haven't I heard about this?"

Tai shrugged. "I have no idea. I thought you knew."

"Oh, this day just gets better and better. First my brother tells me I'm going to die, then my mother tells me I'm going to kill Kyle, then you tell me one of the two is going to happen this Saturday." I paced Tai's room and chewed on my nonexistent fingernails.

"Josh thinks you're going to die?"

I quickly explained Josh's powers and how he saw a vision of my death.

"That's really scary, Priss. I think you should tell your mom. She'll know what to do."

"I can't. Josh isn't ready. I don't want to break his trust."

"How in the world does your mother not know about his powers already?"

I shrugged. "Some secret psychic thing, I guess. It's probably the same way my mom is able to block my super hearing so I can't eavesdrop on her conversations."

"Well maybe you should talk to him again. Get exact details or something. Maybe we can still change the future somehow."

I sat back down on her bed and thought about that for a moment. It was a good plan. If I knew how I was supposed to die, maybe I could avoid that situation.

"Great idea, Tai. You're a genius." I gave her a quick hug and then headed back down the street to my house.

* * *

"Josh, is it possible you're wrong?" I asked, leaning on his door frame and staring into his football-obsessed room. Pittsburgh Steelers posters covered his walls. He had a weight bench in the corner of his room in front of a mirror to help him get closer to his dream of becoming a professional quarterback. I could imagine him working out for hours and then staring at his muscles, probably while listening to "Fighter" by Christina Aguilera. But then I looked a little closer at the weight bench. It was brand-new except for some dust and cobwebs covering it. "Oh my goodness. You've never used this weight bench, have you?"

Staring up at the ceiling he said, "The summer I turned thirteen, I woke up one morning and I had muscles. Just like that. I knew that wasn't normal, so I begged Dad to buy me that weight bench, wore baggy clothes for a month, and pretended to work out every day."

I remembered that. He also grew six inches taller that summer. I didn't think anything of it at the time, but now it all made sense.

"Is that when the visions started?" I dusted off the bench and took a seat.

Josh nodded. "Mom got suspicious at first. She would stare at me constantly like I was some sort of science experiment. So I had to work on suppressing the visions. One day I figured out that mom had some sort of mental powers of her own. She was staring at me, as usual, and then I suddenly felt her in my head. I quickly came up with a way to block her. After that, the visions went away almost completely for two years. I thought I was cured."

"Josh, your abilities are not a disease."

"I just want to be normal. I don't want my mother running off saving the world. I don't want my sister setting things on fire and getting kidnapped by bad guys, and I don't want visions of death invading my mind."

I hated that Josh thought something was wrong with Mom and me. But I *did* want to make him feel better. "Well, maybe you *are* normal. Maybe this is all a coincidence and you don't have powers. Maybe your vision was wrong."

Josh closed his eyes and shook his head. "Everything I see comes true." He sighed. "You were sick, too sick to defend yourself. You get shot. In the chest." He was so sure and so convinced, I felt his vision was a certainty. But it just couldn't be true. There had to be some mistake.

"Maybe it's just a dream, you know. Dreams don't really mean anything. I mean, just last night I dreamt that Charlie turned into a tap-dancing monkey and Chester sold him to the Russian circus."

He opened his eyes and glared at me. "It's not a dream. It's a vision," he said, not finding the humor in my possible explanation. "Don't you think I wish it wasn't true? I've tried to think of every possible logical scenario that doesn't end with your death. Nothing changes. All of my visions have come true. All of them."

"I think you should tell Mom. She can help you decode the vision or something. I bet she can give you some brain exercises or whatever it is psychic people need to do to strengthen their psychicness. If that's a word." I stood up and paced his room. "There's probably so much you can do with your powers. I bet you have no idea what you're capable of."

Josh sat up and crossed his arms. He looked as stubborn as Charlie when Dad tells him he has to finish his broccoli before leaving the table. Chester figured out how to beat the great broccoli battle long ago by shoveling the nasty vegetable into his drink cup. In any case, telling Mom was not an option in Josh's mind. I still couldn't believe she didn't already know. I mean, she knew about my powers almost immediately and even helped me cope with them by sending me the calm feeling.

"So, how have you been able to keep Mom from finding out about you? What's your trick?"

"Christina Aguilera."

What was he talking about? He must not have heard the question.

"No, I said—"

"I know what you said. Christina Aguilera keeps her out of my head. When I feel her entering my mind, I start singing a Christina Aguilera song. She immediately retreats. I don't even think she realizes she does it. She just can't stand pop music. It's like nails on a chalkboard to her."

"Are you serious?" I said, staring at him in disbelief.

"Try it. Works every time."

I'd definitely be trying it. There were lots of thoughts that I'd like to keep private. But my abilities weren't one of them. I kinda needed Mom to help me understand what was going on with my body. And though he didn't realize it yet, so did Josh.

"You really need to talk to Mom. It's not that bad. She can help you."

"Not gonna happen. I don't need help," he said with Charlie-like stubbornness.

"Josh, ignoring your powers won't make them go away."

I sat next to him on his bed and placed my arm on his shoulder. The way he jerked away from me kind of hurt my feelings. He really did think Mom and I were freaks. That's why he didn't want to accept his gift. If he did, it would mean he was just like us.

Chapter 22
Ice Cream Challenge

"Get up; let's go," my mother said at the butt-crack of dawn on Friday morning, a full three hours before I had to be in school. I hadn't woken up that early since I was in gymnastics.

"Go where?"

"It's time to start training."

"Oh, you have got to be kidding me," I said, struggling to open my eyes. But when I looked at her, I knew she was seriously serious. She wore a black catsuit with the same silver belt of gadgets that I'd seen before.

She tossed me a bundle of clothes and then started pulling her hair into a tight bun. "I have to get my hair out of the way. I don't want you accidentally setting it on fire."

"Very funny, Mom. But that wouldn't happen anyway. It's Friday. Just like last month, my powers came on a Saturday and disappeared on a Thursday. I can't set anything on fire. My powers are gone."

My mother pretended she didn't hear me as she walked to the other side of my room with a smirk on her face. I sat up and stretched out the matching black catsuit she'd given me. We were gonna look like a couple of redheaded ninjas. Ridiculous. Then, out of the corner of my eye, I saw my dresser come through the air, straight at me. I caught it just a split second before it flattened me. "What are you doing? You could've taken my head off!"

"Told you. You still have your powers. Now get dressed. We need to finish before the sun comes out."

Seconds later, my father hopped into my room, a crutch in one hand and a pistol in the other. "What's going on?"

"Nothing, honey. Everything's fine. I was just starting Priss' training. You really do overreact sometimes, Greg."

My father let out a sigh of relief. He clicked on the safety to his gun and then jammed it into his boxer shorts.

"Overreact? My daughter was kidnapped less than a week ago. I think I have every right to *overreact* as you call it."

"That's why I need to train her, so it doesn't happen again."

"Excuse me? Happen again?" I asked. "What makes you think it's going to happen again?"

Dad turned around and stormed off—well he kind of hopped off. Storming anywhere is nearly impossible with a broken leg.

"Just get dressed," my mother said before going after him.

Seriously, why did they think it was going to happen again? I was starting to get paranoid. My mother thought I was going to be kidnapped again and my brother was convinced I was going to die. In any case, something bad was going to happen and I needed to be prepared.

My training took place in a clearing in the woods near where we parked our jet. I still couldn't believe my family owned an invisible jet. Freaking awesome. What wasn't awesome was the way my mother kicked my butt repeatedly. She had no mercy for me.

"Priss, suck it up and concentrate. You can beat me."

"No, I can't. You've had years of training. I haven't."

"You have to use your strengths. You may not have my training, but you're creative, feisty, and determined. I've seen you playing those video games. You do whatever it takes to win. You have to have the same attitude in combat. Do whatever it takes."

We resumed our attack positions on opposite sides of the field. She expected me to beat her, a genetically enhanced super weapon, in pitch black darkness after only learning three simple karate moves. She was insane.

She did that super fast running thing where I could barely see her. Any second she was going to kick my legs out from under me or flip me over her shoulder onto my back. It was the same thing over and over again. I was starting to get really annoyed. I retreated into a thicket of bushes, where I got an idea.

"Mom, help! I set the bushes on fire and now I'm trapped. Mommy, get me out of here."

"I'm coming, Prissy!" She ran through the fire to get to me, but when she was close enough, I grabbed her arm, twisted it behind her back, and then pinned her to the ground.

"Touché, Priss. Touché."

"Does that mean I win? Can I go back to sleep now?"

"Okay, that's enough for today. Just let me put this fire out before you burn down the town."

I didn't get to go back to sleep, though. Before I knew it, I was yawning in front of my locker at school.

"Tired?" Kyle asked me at the height of my yawn. I hate when people ask that. First of all, if I'm yawning of course I'm tired. Why else would I be opening my mouth like a Venus Fly Trap? Second of all, it's impossible to interrupt a yawn to answer a question. I was just stuck there with my mouth wide open unable to respond for like five seconds, which feels like five hours when there's a cute boy staring at your uvula. My hands were full of books so I couldn't even cover my mouth. I looked like an idiot.

"Yeah, a little," I said when my yawn finally ended.

"Well, I know what'll wake you up." Kyle sounded very mischievous. What was he up to? I remembered Tai telling me he wanted to kiss me at the River Day Dance. Was he planning on a test kiss right there in the hall? My stomach did a back flip as I stared at his lips. Oh my God, his lips were perfect. "The Ice Cream Challenge," he added, jolting me out of my thoughts.

The Ice Cream Challenge was an ongoing feud between the seventh and eighth grades of Polk Middle. On the last Friday of every month, an eighth grade boy challenged a seventh grade boy to an all-you-can eat ice cream gorging. If the seventh grader won, he and two friends got to sit at the eighth grade tables for a week. If the eighth grader won, then the loser had to be his servant for a week. It was humiliating.

Anyway, after school on the last Friday of the month, all the kitchen staff would run off to cash their pay checks, so the entire student body secretly gathered in the cafeteria to watch the festivities. Each contestant had to stick their head under the soft serve nozzle and fill their faces with ice cream until one of them either puked or surrendered to the brain freeze.

Kyle and I had been training for his turn for weeks, blowing our allowance on cones at Willie's Sweet Shop and racing each other to finish. I beat him every time, but unfortunately, it was an unwritten rule that girls weren't allowed to participate in the ICC. Most girls didn't want to compete for fear of getting ice cream in their hair. And after Lucy Mane puked on the principal's shoes two years ago after her challenge, girls were pretty much banned from the sport.

"That's right! Your challenge is today. How do you feel? Are you ready to kick some eighth grade butt?" I started to get excited. I knew Kyle would win. I mean, he had *me* for a coach. Of course, he'd win.

"Actually, I can't do it. I have an audition in the morning and I can't risk the extra calories."

I rolled my eyes. "Great. Get me all excited for nothing." I shut my locker with my shoulder and struggled to balance my two armloads of books. "So who's taking your place?" I asked as Kyle took the books out of my hands to carry them for me.

"You."

"Me? But ... but I'm a girl."

"I know. That's why I had to slip Jimmy a twenty so he would even take the challenge."

Well, time really flies when you have a date with destiny, and by the time Kyle was done with his pep talks,

I truly felt like defeating Jimmy Vartanian in the Ice Cream Challenge was my destiny. It was like G.I. Joe versus Cobra, like the Autobots versus the Decepticons, or Anybody versus the Yankees. It was your classic good versus evil. The seventh grade just had to win, and it was all up to me.

"Choose your flavor," Jimmy Vee said to me, standing before the ice cream machine moments before the gorging took place.

"Chocolate." That was a psyche-out choice. Most people chose vanilla thinking it would be easier to get down, so Kyle and I decided we would choose chocolate in order to confuse the opponent. Yeah, now that I think about it, that made no sense, but whatever.

The entire cafeteria erupted into screams and cheers after Ashley Martin, the eighth grade president, yelled, "Go," but all I could hear was Kyle's voice.

"Priss has so got this," he was saying.

"You're crazy. She's a girl. Any second she's gonna give up because she doesn't want to get fat," the boy he was talking to replied.

"You have no idea about this girl. She's different. No, she's more than different. She's incredible. She can do anything."

Brain freeze was no longer a possibility as I felt my whole body flush at Kyle's words. The ice cream melted as soon as it got to within an inch of my face and I ended up just drinking chocolate milk. Easy.

With the challenge under control, I let my mind wander. I started imagining Kyle and me at the River Day Dance tomorrow night. I wondered how my first kiss would happen. Would he ask if he could kiss me or would he take me by surprise, turn me around, and dip me like in one of those old Southern movies? I didn't have too much time to wonder as, before I knew it, Kyle pulled me out from under the ice cream machine and said, "It's over, Priss. You won!"

He hugged me tightly, not caring that I smeared chocolate ice cream all over his crisp button-down white shirt. He smelled good, really good, kind of like what I imagined all those gorgeous guys in cologne ads smelled like. And his arms felt so strong around me. When did he get so strong? I felt weak. Kind of like how I felt the other day after he'd walked me home from school. Any second I was going to set something on fire. Probably him. I had to get out of there.

"I gotta go," I said, pushing away from him.

"But why? I thought we could go celebrate your victory. I bought a new video game. You could come over—"

"No way. Not tonight. I gotta go."

"What about the dance tomorrow?" he called after me. I was already halfway out of the door.

"I'll meet you there," I yelled behind me.

I ran out into the hallway, not sure which way to go. I just knew I had to get outta there before sparks flew out of my hands or two tons of chocolate spewed out of my mouth.

I felt weak and hot and nauseated and just plain icky. By the time I reached the parking lot of Polk Middle School, I was so lightheaded I thought I would faint. I tried to concentrate on my meditation techniques, but I couldn't focus. When I closed my eyes, all I saw was Kyle's face. I could feel his arms around me, and I thought I would explode.

Just when I couldn't take it anymore and I thought I would send the whole parking lot up in flames, I felt the refreshingly cool foam of a fire extinguisher.

"Josh? What are you doing here?" I asked, shaking the foam off my hands.

"I knew you were in trouble."

"What? How?"

He shrugged. "I don't know. I just knew."

"What do you mean you just knew?"

"I told you, I don't know. Stop asking questions and get in the car before somebody wonders why I'm shooting you with a fire extinguisher."

He threw a towel at me and then got into his truck. "And don't puke any chocolate ice cream on my seats or I'll kill you."

I wanted to ask him how he knew about the chocolate ice cream but I knew it had to be the same way he knew I needed help. He must have discovered some new aspects of his powers. I decided not to press him about it. Learning about his powers obviously made him really cranky. So, instead, once I got into his truck, I leaned over, gave him a big hug, and said, "Thanks, Josh."

Chapter 23
Mother-Daughter Day

"Priss, get dressed," my mother said early, I mean really early, Saturday morning.

"Oh, this is getting so old so fast," I said, slapping the pillow over my face.

"I'm taking you out. I think it's time we had a mother-daughter day."

"What's that?"

My mother shrugged. "Someone named Oprah said it was a good idea so I thought I'd give it a try."

Hmph. Maybe my mother was going to take a stab at being normal. Maybe we'd spend the day at the mall shopping or doing whatever it was mothers and daughters were supposed to do together. I should've known that wasn't going to happen when my mother put on her silver utility belt over her jeans.

When we ended up on the jet, I still hoped deep down that we were going shopping. Maybe she was taking me to New York or to that big mall in Minnesota. Unfortunately, she didn't go into any details of where we were headed. I put my feet up on the dashboard as my mother told me more about herself.

"I was conceived in a test tube. My DNA was spliced with the genetic make-up of different animals and then enhanced electronically."

"Whoa. Wait. What animals?" I said, taking my feet down and bolting upright.

"Well, many different ones. For example, a cheetah for agility and speed."

"A cheetah? Are you saying I'm part cat?"

"I guess you can say that."

"Great, as if I wasn't strange enough. Instead of pimples, I'm gonna get fleas." I put my feet up again and leaned back in the copilot's seat, hoping to catch a few more minutes of sleep. Unfortunately, I couldn't help listening to her story. It was pretty interesting.

"Anyway, a volunteer soldier served as a surrogate mother and gave birth to me. I never knew who she was. I don't even know her name."

Wow, my mother never had a mother figure. That really helped me understand why she had no idea how to form a true mother-daughter bond. I guess it was something we'd have to figure out together.

My mother cleared her throat, obviously trying to swallow her emotions, and continued. "After I was born, a computer chip was implanted in my brain to further the mutation as I grew. I've had my capabilities since birth, but I'm guessing that since you're second generation, your abilities are manifesting differently. Your dad and I have studied your blood work. Your mutations come from the X chromosome that you inherited from me and were initiated by a spike in your estrogen and pheromone levels."

"Like I understand anything you just said."

"For the life of me, I can't figure out whether you're more powerful than me or not. Logically, since you're only half … mutant, for lack of a better word, you should be weaker. But for God's sake, you can shoot fire out of your fingers. I can't do anything like that. I'm starting to think your genes have mutated further than mine. Maybe my progeny have even more potential than I do. If that's the case, God help us all when the twins go through puberty."

I shuddered at the thought. I didn't want to imagine a super-powered version of Snot Wars.

"So where are we going?" I asked, giving up on getting any sleep.

"Today, we're going on your first mission."

"Whoa. Wait. What? Mission? What do you mean mission?"

"Let me explain—"

"Oh, yes, please explain. I'd love an explanation. And it better involve a mall and a MasterCard."

"Specimen Xi has orders to kill a high-ranking official in Canada." I searched my brain for that name. Should I know this person? Then I remembered what my mother told me about the names of the fighting machines produced by the Selliwood Institute. Specimen Xi must have been one of the more recent ones since Xi was a letter of the Greek alphabet. "I was able to intercept a direct communication from Colonel Selliwood to her," she continued.

"So, why does she want to kill this dude and what does it have to do with me losing my Saturday morning?" I had to admit I was a little more than bitter. I mean, I thought we were supposed to be bonding while shopping or something. Instead she was taking me to work.

"Canada owns the North Pole—"

"Really? Santa is Canadian? Who knew?"

"Apparently," she said, ignoring my little joke, "Colonel Selliwood was doing some illegal research up there and Pierre Marchaud—"

"Who?"

"The high-ranking Canadian official."

"Right."

"Pierre Marchaud found out about it. He ordered the activity to stop, pending further investigation."

I took a deep breath and tried to calm down. I still didn't quite understand what this had to do with me.

Mom apparently read my mind and said, "Xi is only eleven years old. If this comes to hand-to-hand combat, which is highly plausible knowing Xi, things will be much easier if you fight her instead of me. How will a thirty-six-year-old woman look fighting a child? Bystanders might attack me thinking I'm abusing her."

I stared at her in disbelief. How could she not tell me this? Well, I knew why. If I had known her plan before we left Pennsylvania, I never would have gone.

"Sounds like a normal mother-daughter day to me." I closed my eyes again and tried to pretend this was not happening.

We found Pierre Marchaud on an outing with his family at an art museum in Montreal. Completely unaware that he had a pre-teen assassin looking to take him out, he walked from exhibit to exhibit, pointing out boring paintings to his seven-year-old son and five-year-old daughter. Mr. Marchaud wasn't a high enough official to have a large police backing. He only had two bodyguards, who lagged behind him and chatted with his wife. He was an easy target. Sure there were museum guards at various exits, but their average age was about 112. This guy definitely needed us.

"What's probably going to happen," my mother said as we snacked on ham sandwiches across the room from where the Marchauds enjoyed their lunch, "is that Xi will pose as a lost child or something. When a security guard comes to her assistance, she'll grab his weapon, shoot Mr. Marchaud, and then escape without a trace. At least that's how it was done in my day. It might be a little different now, but the main idea is the same. No one will suspect a child."

"I don't think I can do this," I said, placing my barely eaten sandwich back on the plate. My stomach felt worse than when I accidently drank Chester's patented macaroni and paste milkshake.

"Priss, trust me. It's the easiest way. Look at Mr. Marchaud with his children. Do you really want those kids to lose a father? How would you feel if someone threatened me or *your* father?"

I looked over at the Marchaud family again. The little boy was laughing so hard at something his father said that milk flew out of his nose. My mother was right. I couldn't let Xi break up this family all because Selliwood wasn't getting something he wanted. It just wasn't right.

"Okay, I'll do it."

"That's my girl. Now a couple of things you need to know about Xi," she said, leaning in as if about to tell me a girlie secret. "She has no pain receptors, which means she doesn't feel … well … anything. She can also regenerate her flesh and body parts."

"Which means what?"

"It means that if she loses an arm or something, she can just grow it back."

"Great. And I suppose she's had martial arts training since the time she started walking, just like you."

"Well, yes."

"Anything else?"

"Yes, she's a sadistic psychopath who enjoys watching other people's pain since she can't feel any of her own— and she just arrived."

I whipped my head around and saw a stylish little Chinese girl with long, curly black hair and fluorescent blue highlights enter the museum café. She must have spent hours getting her hair to curl like that. And highlights? Who let an eleven-year-old get highlights? I was so jealous.

Xi stopped for a second, pulled a lipstick out of her purse, and then made her lips cherry red. Makeup too? I was totally jealous. Dad said I couldn't wear makeup or dye my hair until I was sixteen!

One thing was for sure. This girl was completely vain. Maybe I could use that to my advantage.

Her red two-inch heels clicking all the way, she strode right up to the Marchauds' table and then stopped and stared at them with a cold, blank expression. A really awkward moment followed in which the Marchauds looked back and forth between each other, trying to figure out who knew the creepy yet stylish little Chinese girl standing at the end of their table.

"Are you lost, little girl?" I heard Mrs. Marchaud ask. This caught the attention of one of the bodyguards, who stood and put his hand on Xi's shoulder. A sinister smile crawled across her face as if this was the cue she was waiting for. She grabbed the guard's arm and flipped him over her shoulder, completely destroying the table. I ran over just as Xi reached for his gun. As she aimed at Mr. Marchaud's head, I sent a blast of fire that melted the gun right there in her hand. Xi just stared at the burning metal. It had no effect on her.

Screams erupted in the café. The Marchaud family rushed out with their bodyguards as others ran for cover.

"You should not have done that, Priscilla Sumner," she said slowly with a strong British accent. "No one gets in my way." How did she know my name? I didn't have too much time to think about that as she picked up a round table and tossed it at my head as if she was flicking a playing card. I ducked out of the way then did a round-off into a back flip toward her. When close enough, I went to sweep her legs out, but she'd already done a flip out of the way.

"Oh this should be fun. I'll get to kill two people in one day. Splendid." She whipped off her purse and twirled the metal chain in the air while doing a flip over my head. The next thing I knew, her purse chain was around my neck.

"I think I'll kill you slowly. Make you gasp and beg for air. Are you ready to beg, Priss?" she said, stretching the cord tight from behind me.

She was choking the life out of me. I grabbed her forearms and burned her, but she didn't feel a thing.

Her skin actually grew back before my eyes. She was indestructible.

Xi pulled the chain tighter and tighter. I started to see spots. *Mom, where are you?*

I'm here, Priss, she answered

I need your help. I can't beat her alone.

Yes, you can. Get creative. You can do this. I'll be here if you need me. I won't let anything happen to you.

My mind drifted as I stared down at Xi's awesome red shoes. I wondered if they were Jimmy Choos. I'd heard those were really expensive. No matter what they were, they matched her stylish black miniskirt and red and black silk shirt perfectly. She looked like she'd just stepped off the cover of *Teen Tramp* magazine. That's when I got an idea. I reached behind me and put one hand on her shirt and one on her skirt. She might not be able to feel pain, but she could certainly feel the embarrassment of standing buck naked in the middle of a museum café. I mean, take away the assassin, and she was just a preteen girl like any other.

Her expensive silk clothes burned quickly. Xi screamed and tried to cover with her hands what her clothes once had. "I'll get you for this, Priss!" she yelled as she ran away.

I fell to my knees, gasping for air. Once I could breathe again, I thought about what just happened. Did I just defeat a genetically enhanced super human? I was about to pump my fists and do a celebratory dance when I noticed people were still hiding behind chairs and staring at me like they were terrified. I started to assure them that everything was okay when suddenly I felt like I was flying. Everything blurred as if I was traveling at light speed or something.

By the time I figured out what was going on, Mom and I were back at the jet.

"God, that hurt!" I said, clutching my head.

"Sorry, about that. I had to get us out of there before the police showed up." She bounded the steps of the jet, leaving me wobbling behind her. No wonder Dad lost consciousness whenever she did the superfast running thing with him. I mean, I had half her genes and I still felt like I could pass out from it.

"That was excellent work for your first mission, Priss," she said, sitting down in the pilot's seat. "I'm extremely proud of you. You kept your cool. You got creative and thought outside the box. But let's consider what you could have done differently."

"What do you mean?" I said, making myself comfy in the copilot's seat and closing my eyes. I had just saved a man's life. Was she really going to critique me? "I won, Mom. What does it matter?"

"Oh it definitely matters, Priss. Just because you won doesn't mean there isn't room for improvement. Don't succumb to overconfidence. No matter how good you think you are, there's always someone better."

"Way to suck the joy out of my mood, Mom."

"I just want you to be prepared. Xi has about eleven more years of training than you. You got lucky today and you had me there for backup. The next time you fight her—"

"Whoa, wait, what do you mean next time?"

"You think this is over? No, way. Xi will be back for revenge. You can count on it."

Chapter 24

First Kiss?

On the way back from Canada, I decided to pick my mom's brain about what to do with Kyle. I mean, my first kiss was only a few hours away, and I was still in danger of frying him.

"So, about that whole sex video thing."

"Uh huh," my mother said, not taking her eyes off the sky.

"Well, I totally don't need it." She stole a glance at me and then returned her attention back to flying. "But if I did, what kind of things would it teach me?"

She took a deep breath and then said, "Hold out your left hand." When I did it, she added, "Show me a flame."

I concentrated on that little part in my brain that brought the heat. The flames appeared above each of my finger tips.

"Now shut off all your fingers except your index finger."

I had to think about this one for a little bit. I'd never tried to control each finger individually. After a few seconds, I'd done it. One single flame hovered above my index finger.

"Now shut that off and turn on your ring finger."

That was even harder to do. My ring finger flame was probably the weakest. But, once again, with a little focus and concentration, I got it to work. I even made the flame grow so it was as strong as the others were.

"What are you doing each time to turn on the flame?" my mother asked.

I explained to her about the little key in my brain and how I turn it in order to bring the heat.

"These exercises will help you develop your ability to control your powers and your skill at using them. You are obviously mentally capable of shutting your powers on and off, which is why you thought they went away with your period. I think you're a little young, but if you plan on kissing Kyle, I suggest you make sure your flame is off. You also might want to keep your hands in your pockets the first couple of times."

I thought about this. It didn't sound too hard. *I'll just put my hands behind my back or something while Kyle kisses me tonight. Tonight. Oh my God, it is happening tonight.*

Suddenly, I felt something strange going on in my head. I glared at my mother. She stared out into the sky, pretending she had no idea she was entering my mind. I started humming the first Christina Aguilera song I could think of. My mother rolled her eyes and retreated. I just hoped she hadn't learned anything about my plans for the night.

* * *

"I can't believe you're doing this for me," I said as Tai climbed through my window that night. Well, she tried to climb. Poor girl had zero upper body strength. I ended up picking her up and placing her in my room. "I mean, you should be going to the dance with Spencer."

"What are friends for? You have a guaranteed kiss coming from Kyle. I'm not even that into Spencer. His sloppy hair annoys me. Plus, a black person square dancing is just wrong on so many levels."

Given my dad's history of overprotectiveness (is that a word?), we decided that the only guaranteed way for me to get out of the house to see Kyle was to sneak out. Tai was going to be my body double, putting on a red wig and hiding under the covers. I'd laid the groundwork all day by talking about how tired I was and how badly I just wanted to go to bed early. It was a perfectly believable story given that I'd flown to Canada and back and defeated a genetically enhanced assassin.

At about six o'clock, I faked some back pain and headed to bed. Josh gave me a skeptical look. He knew I was lying, but thankfully, he didn't blow my cover. He was probably too afraid I'd tell Mom about his powers.

"So, you sure you're ready for this? You're not gonna kill Kyle or anything," Tai said, adjusting the wig on her head. She looked absolutely ridiculous with red hair.

"I think I'm good. My mom gave me some tips. Plus, you should have seen what I did to that Xi girl today. It was such an adrenaline rush. I feel like I can do anything."

"You're starting to like this superhero thing, aren't you?"

"I think it's what I'm meant to do."

"And you thought you and your mom had nothing in common," she said with a smile. I guess she was right about that. After spending the day with my mom, I felt like I had a purpose in life. I kind of understood why my mother spent so much time away from us. Lives were at stake. I couldn't imagine how devastated those two kids would have been to see their father get his brains blown out. "So how did you and your mom get out of there without making the six o'clock news or something?"

"My mom totally took care of that. She scrambled some electrical wavelength or something so that cell phones and cameras wouldn't work during the whole ordeal. There were only word-of-mouth reports, and by the time the news cameras arrived, half the people said two robots were fighting and the other half swore it was two aliens. The news just wrote it off as a ridiculous publicity stunt from the museum. My mom is a genius."

* * *

Tai was right about another thing ,too. Square dancing is just wrong, period, no matter who's doing it. Kyle and I spent the first half hour just pointing and laughing at our neighbors in their pioneer outfits. Amazingly, both of us had shown up in regular clothes. I wore a cute, ruffly, red baby doll top; a pair of straight-leg jeans; and my favorite white knit sweater with little red embroidered hearts on the sleeve. Kyle looked like he just stepped off the cover of a magazine in his black button-down shirt, loose-fitting black jeans, and pale yellow tie.

"You want to get out of here?" he asked after we couldn't laugh anymore. "Let's go for a walk."

I smiled and nodded, unable to utter a sound. *Is it going to happen now? I thought he would wait until the hay ride after the dance, but now that I think about it, that wouldn't be a good idea. I'd probably set the hay on fire. No, a nice walk under the stars would be perfect.*

"I'm glad you came. I was afraid you'd stand me up. You've been pretty weird lately," he said as we headed toward town square. I knew exactly where we were going. The gazebo at the center of town was decorated with twinkle lights for the River Day celebration. It was the absolute perfect spot for a kiss.

"Yeah, sorry about that. I got kinda sick after the Ice Cream Challenge and I didn't want you to see me puke."

"I wouldn't have cared. I've seen you puke before."

"Really, when?"

"Easter. Fifth grade. We raced each other to see who could eat the most marshmallow Peeps. You won, but then you puked all over my brand-new saddle shoes."

"Oh my God, I forgot about that. Sorry about the shoes."

"Are you kidding? I hated those shoes. That was the biggest favor you could've done for me."

We both laughed as we stepped inside the lighted gazebo. That's when the nervous silence came. And now with my mind full of memories of chocolate ice cream and marshmallow Peeps, I was starting to get nauseous again.

"You're really beautiful," he said after a few minutes.

"Me? Beautiful?" I couldn't believe he'd said that. No one had ever called me beautiful before.

Kyle reached for my hand and pulled me close to him. "You have the prettiest eyes I've ever seen on anyone ever." He touched the side of my face with his free hand. He still smelled amazing, and his hand was so soft and warm. I hoped my hand wasn't too warm. I didn't want to burn him. Just in case, I slipped my hand out of his and jammed my fingers into my pockets.

He closed his eyes and leaned toward me. It was happening. It was really happening. I was going to have my first kiss. Amazingly, I wasn't nervous anymore. I felt … comfortable, like Kyle was the best friend I never knew I always had. We'd known each other our entire lives, and though for most of that time we were fighting, I think that was because we were so alike.

I searched my mind to check my fire switch. The closer Kyle got to me and the more his sexy scent filled my nostrils, the harder it was to keep the switch in the off position. He kept turning me on. My fingers burned a hole through my jeans. *Think cool thoughts. Think cool thoughts.*

I closed my eyes and could almost feel his soft lips on mine when suddenly I heard my mother yell my name frantically. I gave an annoyed groan and opened my eyes. How was I supposed to kiss a boy with my mother talking in my head?

Kyle continued leaning forward, and his lips landed in my ear after I'd turned away. "Is something wrong?" He breathed into his hand for a breath check, thinking that was the reason for my sudden disinterest in kissing.

I thought about that question for a moment. My mother's voice sounded panicked. My mother never panicked. I felt as though something *was* wrong.

I pushed Kyle away and searched my brain for my mother's voice. Nothing. There was nothing. I called Josh's name in my head, hoping maybe he had the same type of telepathy as my mother and could tell me if something was wrong. Once again, nothing. I tried not to panic. I mean, it's not like I'd ever communicated with Josh telepathically before. Why would I suddenly be able to now? But, for some reason, I just had a really bad feeling. I had to get home.

"I gotta go," I told Kyle, running out of the gazebo.

"Go? Why? What did I do?" he asked, but I was already in a full sprint back to my house.

I knew something was definitely up when I saw a helicopter circling in the sky, but it was so much worse than I ever imagined.

Chapter 25

Gamma Girl

I ran into Tai's house so I could get a good look without being seen. Two black Hummers were parked in front of my house. Men with guns stood beside the vehicles: guards from the Selliwood Institute. I watched in horror as they dragged my father through the front door with a gun pointed to his head. Next they forced my mother out. She had a glowing collar around her neck like one of those flea collars you put on dogs. I assumed the collar kept her from using her powers. Otherwise, all those men would be lying in a pile of pain.

Next my brothers were escorted out. How could they point a gun at five-year-olds? Tears swelled in my eyes.

"Just do what they say. Everything will be fine," Josh whispered to the twins. But my little brothers were never known for their obedience. As soon as they could, they broke free and ran towards the guards who held my mother and father. They kicked the guards in the shins and pelted them with little punches.

The guards raised their guns and aimed. I gasped. They were going to shoot my baby brothers!

Then an ominous figure emerged from between the Hummers. He was dressed in a black uniform with gold shiny buttons. He raised his hand, and the guards immediately dropped the weapons aimed at my brothers. "Not here," he said.

Not here? What did he mean by that?

"Gregory and Quindolyn Sumner," he said so loud I had to tone down my super hearing, "you are hereby under arrest for treason and terrorism." Whoa, wait. I recognized that voice. When I was tied to a chair at the Selliwood Institute, a male voice said I had to die. This was the voice.

"That's a load of bull, Selliwood, and you know it," my father yelled just before a guard rammed a gun into his stomach. My dad fell to his knees. My mother tried to punch the guard, but her arm froze in midair. She too fell to her knees. I thought I saw her grimace in pain.

"Colonel Selliwood, we have a problem," a guard said, standing in the doorway of my house. "When we went for the girl, we found this instead." He presented a scared and shivering Tai.

"Great," Colonel Selliwood said sarcastically.

"How would you like to precede, Colonel?"

"Specimen Gamma!" he called. After a series of flips across my front lawn, a lean figure dressed in a dark blue spandex outfit with jet black hair down to her waist landed in front of the colonel. She looked about twenty years old.

"Find her and meet us at the institute. And don't underestimate her. She's probably just as powerful as you."

"Yes, Colonel Selliwood. I will not fail."

I almost wet myself.

Then something strange happened. One by one the guards turned their guns on Colonel Selliwood. Maybe my mother had figured out a way to override the collar and was now controlling them.

"What's going on?" Colonel Selliwood asked, a hint of terror in his voice. "Stand down; that's an order." The guards didn't listen.

"Sir, it's the boy," the Gamma Girl volunteered after staring at Josh. "He's a telepath. He's using some sort of hypnotic suggestion."

"Restrain him."

Gamma did a back flip over to my brother. After a kick to his face sent him reeling backward, she placed a knee into his chest, pinning him to the ground, and slapped a collar around his neck. The guards immediately dropped their weapons. After shaking their heads a couple of times like wet puppies trying to dry off, they went back to tormenting my family.

Josh groaned and rolled around on the grass. Poor Josh. His first attempt at really using his powers had failed painfully.

My mother closed her eyes and turned her head, not able to tolerate the sight of her son bleeding and writhing on the ground. My father tried to lunge forward and attack, but given his handcuffs and broken leg, he was quickly subdued.

I ducked below the window, afraid that any second the scary Gamma girl would spot me. As I blinked away tears, I tried to calm my brain and think rationally. What would my mother do? *Tell me what to do, Mom. Please tell me.* Though I'd told her repeatedly to stay out of my head, I now wished with all my heart that I could hear her voice in my mind.

I heard the cars drive away with my family and best friend, but I couldn't move. I tried not to even breathe too loudly for fear the killing machine standing outside my house would hear me and come after me.

After what felt like forever, I was finally able to calm the wild beating of my heart and formulate a plan. I had to go save my family. There was no way around it. This Selliwood creep would kill them if I didn't do something. I had to get to the jet, fly to the institute, break in, rescue my family, and then break out. Simple, huh? Not quite. I had no way of even getting into the jet. It was invisible right now. The only thing I knew that made it appear was the button on my mom's silver utility belt. And where was that belt? I closed my eyes and remembered the last time I saw the belt was that morning on our trip to Canada. I remembered exactly where she put it when we came home. I took a deep breath and tried to calm my nerves. I knew what was happening next. It was time for me to go where no Sumner child had ever gone before.

Chapter 26

In the Basement

I lifted myself up slightly and peeked out the window. No sight of Gamma. I tried to imagine what my run-in with her would be like. She was a bit older than Xi. Did that mean she would be even meaner and more trained? I wondered if I even had a chance. I tried not to dwell on it, though. Nothing would stop me from saving my family. I tuned my ears and tried to listen for whatever a killing machine was supposed to sound like. Nothing.

I took a deep breath and dashed out of Tai's house, toward mine. I decided to go to the back door in hopes of avoiding Gamma in case she was staking out the front door.

I slipped into my house as quietly as possible in case she had super hearing as well and then focused on the ominous basement door. All my life, the basement had been completely off-limits. At different times growing up, that place scared me more than the Boogieman and that scary guy with the hockey mask in those horror movies put together. But now my family's survival depended on me going into that terrifying place. I had to swallow my fear.

I touched the doorknob and twisted it. Amazingly, it was open. *Hmph. Maybe this is going to be easier than I thought.* But when I opened the door, I found a metal wall. I didn't see another doorknob or button to push or anything that might move the wall.

Great. Now what?

I'm sure given an hour or so to study the door and its surroundings I would have found the secret box and figured out the secret code to open up the secret wall. But I didn't have that kind of time. So, I did the only thing I could think of. I took a few steps back, got a running start, and rammed into the wall. It moved. A lot. And though my shoulder was pretty sore, I took another few steps back and did it again. This time I got through and ended up falling down the stairs into the basement.

Instantly, an alarm started blaring. My father's face appeared on the huge wall-sized computer. I heard his voice saying, "Intruder, prepare to surrender. Intruder, prepare to surrender." Then the floor underneath where I sat lit up and I heard what sounded like an engine beginning to rev. I looked up and a huge, I mean mega-huge, gun hung from the ceiling and pointed at me.

"Intruder, prepare to surrender. Intruder, prepare to surrender."

"I'm not an intruder. I'm your daughter," I yelled, thrusting myself off of the floor and to a new location. It didn't matter where I stood, though; the floor beneath me lit up and the gun repositioned itself directly at my head.

To my left, I saw what I guessed was my father's gun collection. Dozens of guns of every shape and size were on display in a glass case. Straight ahead, underneath the big computer screen, was what looked like a laboratory with microscopes and test tubes. To my right, my mother's cat suits in white, red, black, and blue hung in a line on the wall. And at the end of the wall was her silver utility belt. I just needed to grab it and get out as fast as possible. As I ran and lunged for the belt, two things happened almost simultaneously. The gun fired, blowing up the place where I was just standing, and Gamma girl flipped into the basement.

I secured the belt around my waist and then took my attack position in preparation to fight Gamma. The beautiful Latin-looking warrior stood about ten feet away from me and whipped out a long stick that had been tucked into a strap on her back. It kind of reminded me of Darth Maul's double light saber, except it didn't glow. She started twirling that thing around, flipping through the air like some sort of acrobatic samurai, and somehow avoiding the blasts coming from the gun in the ceiling.

When she thrust her stick at me, I dodged it and then flipped out of the way, all the while keeping one eye on the gun above us and the other on her.

She shoved her stick at me again and this time nailed me in the nose. God, it was painful. My vision got all fuzzy for a second. I thought I was going to pass out. I felt something warm and wet dripping from my nose. I looked down and saw the blood stains on my cute white knit sweater. *Oh, no you didn't. It is so on.*

The floor beneath me lit up again. I reached up to stop the bleeding with one hand while doing a standing back flip to avoid a sweep technique from Gamma.

I pulled out a throwing star from my mother's utility belt and chucked it at her head. She dodged left, ducking her head right into where I sent a stream of fire. I scorched her hair. Needless to say, she wasn't too happy about this. With a nerve-racking war cry that could make Attila the Hun pee his pants, she came at me again.

This time her stick landed in my gut, causing me to double over in pain. I landed on my hands and knees. I quickly rolled out of the way to avoid a kill from Gamma. I scurried underneath a lab table, trying to catch my breath and get my bearings. That's when I noticed something ... strange. When I fell to the ground, I'd left a bloodied hand print on the floor. That hand print literally dissolved before my eyes. It was like the sensory floor absorbed my blood. The floor powered down. The gun disengaged.

"Priscilla, get out of the basement," my dad's voice said through the computer. "You're going to get yourself killed."

That's exactly what I'm trying to avoid.

Dad must have built in a safety that turned off the gun if the computer sensed one of his kids in the room.

I leaped out from under the table and attacked Gamma. I hoped since I didn't have to worry about getting shot anymore, I could put all of my concentration into defeating her.

I blocked each thrust of her stick with my arms. When I saw an opening, I aimed for her nose with an upper cut just like in Josh's old *Mortal Kombat* game. Blood streamed out of her nose and dripped to the floor, lighting up where she stood. The gun revved again and pointed at her. It must have tested her blood and realized she wasn't a Sumner.

"Priscilla, get out of the basement. You're in danger," my dad's computerized voice said. *Well, duh.*

Gamma flipped away from the lit up floor and landed behind me. She kicked me in the back, sending me face-first into the wall. I turned around just in time to see her aiming that stick right for my head. I grabbed the end of it and flung her against the wall. Then I picked her up by her right arm and leg, spun around, and threw her to the other side of the room.

She hit the wall with a thud. Apparently shocked by how strong I was, she took a second to clear her head and get herself together. That one split-second hesitation was too much. The aerial gun aimed at her and fired. I was already up the stairs when I heard her cry out in pain.

I didn't have time to feel sorry for her. I took off running toward the jet. I had a family to save.

Chapter 27
Stupid Henchmen

I found the Selliwood Institute just where I'd left it, hidden in the side of a mountain in Colorado. I landed the jet in a cave to the south of the warehouse entrance that I'd blown up the week before. I poked around the computer in the console to see if I could find any information that would help me on this rescue mission. I pressed several buttons but only figured out how to make a cup of coffee and start a holographic game of *Tetris*.

I slammed my head down on the keyboard that slid out of the console. *What was I thinking? I'm not smart enough to do this. Maybe if I had Tai by my side or something, she'd be able to handle the technological aspects. But I don't have her. In fact, I might never see her again if I don't figure out what to do and save her with the rest of my family.*

I took some deep, cleansing breaths like my mother had taught me for meditation, and I tried to focus. I thought about the last time I was in the institute and tried to recall as much of it as I could.

It didn't work. All I remembered was the cold, stainless steel room, a couple of unremarkable hallways, and the secret passageway that my father used to get me out. Not very helpful considering I had already blown up that wing of the building.

I tried not to panic as I searched my brain for an answer, but as time ticked on, I felt myself losing hope. Tears leaked from my eyes, and my throat tightened when, suddenly, it hit me. I sat up and looked around. Wiping the tears from my face, I remembered that right here in this very jet, my mother had shown me an image of the institute. She showed me the central control room. If I could bring that image back to my mind and do the mental equivalent of a zoom out on the picture, I'd have a complete blue print of the facility.

Thinking it would help jog my memory, I transferred from the pilot's seat to the copilot's seat where I had been sitting when she showed me. I focused on the central control room, its one entrance and exit, and the dozens of computers that lined the walls. Then I pulled back and saw the featureless corridors coming into view like a world slowly being built in *The Sims*.

Once I knew the layout of the institute, I felt a little more confident about what I had to do. I still didn't know exactly where my family and Tai were located, but at least it was better than going in blind. I exited the jet and ran toward Selliwood.

My instincts kicked in as soon as I saw the armed men standing guard at the entrance. I hid behind a tank and planned my next move.

"I don't know why we're still here," one of the guards said. "I'm supposed to be on vacation. It's just a twelve-year-old girl. She's no match for all of us. I don't care what shoots out of her fingers."

"Well, she did escape from us last week," another one of them said.

"That's because she had Specimen Q with her. She doesn't have a chance on her own."

"Speaking of Specimen Q, what are they going to do to her?"

"Not sure, but it's bound to be painful. She's in the Detaining Quarters."

"Sheesh. I wonder if they're gonna let her live."

"I doubt it."

Detaining Quarters? That didn't sound good. I searched the blue print in my mind and found the Detaining Quarters located in the North Wing of the Institute. I could follow a heating conduit straight there. But first, I had to get into the building.

I took aim and set three tanks on fire off in the distance. Then I hopped into the one I hid behind and started it up. Once it got going, I jumped out and ran in the opposite direction. The guards who weren't distracted by the fire turned and started shooting at the moving tank. At that point, I didn't even have to run for the entrance. I just strolled in through the front door.

Stupid henchmen.

The heating conduit was just wide enough for me to crawl into. I inched along through a heat so intense a normal human would have been dead in minutes. Thank goodness I wasn't normal.

I made it about a hundred yards into the building when my sweater snagged a nail shooting out of the wall. I tried to tug it free, but it just got more caught up. I didn't want to burn the stuck part away and ruin my sweater. I was still hoping Dad would somehow be able to wash out the blood stains and save it the same way he saved Josh's football uniform after the twins wrote a threatening letter to the Teletubbies on it with a Sharpie.

The conduit was too narrow for me to easily squirm out of the sweater. I was working up a sweat trying to wiggle free. Finally, I just stopped moving, took a deep breath and tried to relax. That's when I heard Colonel Selliwood's voice.

"… experts in combat. They can defeat any opponent."

"So where are all these specially trained soldiers? Why haven't I seen them in action?" another voice said.

With a determined burst of energy, I finally twisted myself out of the sweater. Once out, I was easily able to free it from the nail. Then I crawled toward the voices. I looked through a vent and down into the room. It must have been Colonel Selliwood's personal office.

"Mr. President, you've been in office for less than a year. I know you've had a busy start. I didn't want to bore you with unnecessary details. Your predecessor was completely satisfied with my work," Selliwood said to the president's face on his computer screen. They were having some sort of digital meeting. I knew I needed to find my family, but I kinda felt like this was about to be a very important conversation.

"My predecessor has nothing to do with this. I don't know what kind of arrangement you had with him, but I'd like to see with my own eyes what kind of operation you're running. I can be there in the morning to have a face-to-face with these supposedly unstoppable fighting machines," the president said.

"Mr. President, I'd hate for you to go through so much trouble. I—"

"Trouble? Do you want to know what troubles me, Colonel? These soldiers, whom I've never met, cost a reported $3 billion each in training."

Selliwood was silent as I watched the president flip through some papers on his desk. "Forty-two years and $140 billion, yet I'm not aware of a single one of your so-called missions or how they've helped our country."

"Sir, secrecy is imperative to our success and efficiency. Our operations are highly classified."

"Highly classified? Do you know who you're talking to?"

"Yes, Mr. President. I apologize, sir."

They stared at each other in a battle of wills for a few seconds. Finally, the president said, "I'm pulling your funding immediately. You are no longer a government-sponsored agency. When you can prove your necessity to this administration, maybe I'll reconsider."

"Mr. President, you don't know what you're doing. I assure you this outfit is vital to the safety of the country."

"I assure you, Colonel Selliwood, I know exactly what I'm doing. I'm taking the money you're wasting and placing it where it can do some actual good. You no longer work for the United States government. Do I make myself clear?"

"Yes, Mr. President."

Colonel Selliwood turned off his computer and spun his chair around so that I could see his face. I expected him to be totally ticked after that tongue-lashing, but instead that arrogant jerk just smiled maliciously.

"I think the president needs to know exactly how essential my research is," he said to the dark emptiness of his room.

"Don't you mean *our* research?" I nearly jumped out of my skin at the sound of Mr. Witherall's voice. I didn't realize anyone else was in the room. I craned my neck and saw that he was sitting in a recliner in the corner.

"You know what we have to do," Colonel Selliwood continued.

"Nine months ahead of schedule?"

"The president has left me no choice."

"Well, then I better get to work on the final calculations." Mr. Witherall stood. "I'll see you at Crang."

I didn't know what Crang was or just what Selliwood and Witherall *had* to do, but I knew I needed to stop them. First, I needed to save my family.

* * *

After five more minutes of crawling through heating ducts, I found my parents in a stainless steel room similar to the one I was in a few days ago. I looked in on them through a vent. My father was tied to a chair, his eyes bloodied and swollen shut. His face was almost unrecognizable from all the bruises.

My mother appeared fine physically, but she still had the glowing collar around her neck and she was attached to some contraption that obviously put her in an excruciating amount of pain. Probes and electrodes poked out of everywhere while her head hung forward limply.

What was worse was that my brothers and Tai were in the next room separated only by a glass window. They were forcing them to watch my parents' torture.

Tai screamed and started crying when the gun from a guard made contact with my father's face. Josh hugged the twins closer. My mother didn't move. She had to be unconscious to not react to the attack on Dad. *Please don't die, Mom. I'm here. I'm going to save you.*

I found the wires that sent electricity to the room and burned through them instantly shutting off the lights.

"Josh, what's happening?" I heard Charlie cry.

Tears instantly welled in my eyes. I wanted let them know that everything was going to be okay but I couldn't give away my location. I still needed the element of surprise in order to defeat the guards. In the complete blackness, I dropped through the ceiling and landed on one of the brutes who had been abusing my parents.

"Get it off me! Get it off me!" he cried as I rained punches on his head.

"I can't see anything. What's going on?" the other one cried before firing his weapon toward us. I felt a stinging sensation in my arm right before the guard collapsed beneath me. I felt for his pulse. He was dead. Shot by his own friend.

"Ray, you there?" the guard said as I quietly crawled toward the sound of his voice. I could still hear the twins and Tai crying in the background. "You guys shut up over before I shoot you!," he said.

That so was not going to happen.

I swept his legs out from under him. He fell to the ground with a thud. I kicked his gun away then picked him up and flung him against the wall. I knew he was unconscious. I threw him so hard he might've been dead. No one tortures my family like that.

I burned through my father's ropes and then went to disconnect my mother from the device that had immobilized her.

"Good work, Priss," Dad said before passing out. I laid him next to mom and then went to get Josh and Tai.

"Stand back," I yelled at the window before kicking through the glass.

I tried to swallow back emotion as I hugged my brothers and my best friend. This wasn't over. Once I had gotten everyone to safety maybe then I'd have time to cry tears of relief and joy. Until then, I was in fighter mode.

"Josh, carry Mom. Tai, hold the twins' hands," I commanded before picking up Dad. I knew we couldn't go back the way I came. They wouldn't be able to handle the heat. Instead, I lead everyone through the darkness and intricate pathways and halls of the Selliwood Institute. Even amidst the sirens and blinking emergency lights signifying someone had escaped, the guards never caught up with us. I blasted through walls, melted glass, and basically destroyed anything that got in our way until we reached freedom.

When we were almost back at the jet, I noticed my mother coming around.

"Get the others," she whispered. "Save the children."

"Everyone's here, Mom. Me, Dad, Josh, Tai, and the twins. I saved everyone."

"No, the children. Save the children."

"What children?"

"She means the children in the institute," Tai volunteered. "We saw them. There's a bunch of them all wearing inhibitors."

"Do you remember where?"

Tai shook her head.

"Think, Tai. I need a name or something. Did you see a sign or anything?"

"I'm sorry. I can't—" I thought I saw tears welling in her eyes as she shook her head frantically. "What a minute. East. I remember something about east."

"The east wing?"

She nodded. "Yeah, I think that could be it."

I searched the blue print in my mind for the east wing and found something called the Containment Room. That had to be it. "I'm going back in," I said, setting my dad on the ground. "Tai, try to figure out how to get those collars off of Josh and Mom."

"Priss, don't." Josh gave me a knowing look. I knew he was thinking of his vision of my death, but I couldn't let his worries stop me. There were kids in there, kids just like me, and they deserved a chance at a normal life. I wouldn't be able to live with myself if I passed up this opportunity to help them.

Josh rested my mother's limp body on the ground and then tried to block my path. He crossed his arms and puffed out his chest as if he stood a chance against me. "You're not strong enough to stop me, Josh, so you might as well get out of my way." He knew I was right. His shoulders slumped a little as he stepped aside to let me pass.

Before I got two steps away, I felt a hand on my arm. Josh pulled me into a hug and said, "Be careful."

Chapter 28

Fighting *Dirty*

Getting back into to the facility wasn't as easy as I thought. I checked the blue print in my mind as I circled the building. Every entrance had twice as many guards as before. Another distraction of tank fires probably wouldn't work. They'd be on to that by now. If I had super speed I might be able to run right past them like Mom. But I didn't have super speed, and no amount of sitting around and wishing would bring it about. If my mom was conscious, she'd probably tell me to not dwell on what I didn't have or couldn't change. I needed to focus and use my strengths.

I closed my eyes and studied the blueprints again. Maybe I'd missed something. There had to be another way in. Suddenly, I noticed a helicopter launching pad on the roof in the blue print. If they boarded helicopters from the roof, there had to be a way to inside the building from the roof.

With the image still fresh in my mind, I found an isolated corner of the building between the north and west wings and then scaled a drainpipe to the roof. I ran past the two helicopters on the launching pad and toward a door that led to an emergency stairwell. I tried to open the door, but, of course, my life couldn't be that easy. Not only was it locked and fire proof, but the reinforced steel was really going to do a number on my shoulder if I tried to bust through it. My shoulder still ached from ramming through the wall of my basement. I mean, I'm strong, but I'm not invincible. I was just a kid. I should've been home trading baseball cards, or playing video games, or picking out a tasty lip gloss that my boyfriend would enjoy.

Near tears, I put my head in my hands. This was too much. I couldn't do it. But then suddenly, I felt very selfish. No matter how tired I was right now or how much my shoulder hurt, my life was a breeze compared to what those Selliwood kids had probably endured. I could practically hear my mother's voice telling me to suck it up and do whatever it takes. That was just what I was going to do.

I took a few steps back in order to get a running start and crush the door. Just then, I heard footsteps and voices. I looked around and there was nowhere to hide. Without thinking, I flung myself over the side of the building, and held on to the edge with one hand. Once out of sight, I heard the door slam open. Someone was angry.

"I don't understand why we're leaving. We can't let her get away." I heard Xi's distinctive British accent. I pulled myself up slightly and peered over the edge. Xi was storming toward one of the helicopters, followed by Witherall and two more specimens.

"Calm down, Xi. It's not worth it. She's probably long gone by now anyway. We need to concentrate on the next phase," Witherall said.

"I just want to concentrate on pummeling that little red-headed rodent." Xi took off her purse and wrapped the strap around her hand. I could tell she wanted to rearrange my face with her fist. Honestly, I wanted to hop up there and scorch her psychotic tail again, but that wouldn't be wise for several reasons. First, she had two other specimens with her and they were huge. I'd never fought more than one specimen at a time. I wouldn't have a chance. Second, I didn't have time to go into some petty revenge fight when there were children to save.

The door into the building was wide open. Xi had slammed it open so hard that it got stuck for a few seconds. As Witherall and the specimens lifted off in one of the helicopters, the door slowly creaked closed. I waited as long as I could without risking the door shutting, and then I hurled myself onto the roof and made a mad dash for it.

* * *

The children were in another stainless steel room and guarded by three armed men. They stood in attack positions with their weapons engaged. I took a deep breath and then leapt from my hiding place. One of the guards shot off a couple of rounds before I had a chance to melt their weapons with three quick blasts of fire.

I raised my leg in a side kick that connected with a muscular chest over a pair of ribs. I felt his bones crush under the blow. I didn't want to think about the pain he was in as I grabbed the arm of the second guard, twisted it, and shoved him into the third. When he rebounded, I did a windmill kick that landed on his head, sending him to La-La Land. Unfortunately, this gave enough time for the third guard to get off the floor and come up behind me. He wrapped his arms around me and held me in a death grip. Hello? Didn't he get the memo? I can shoot fire out of my finger. I grabbed his arms, burning his flesh. He screamed in pain and then released me. I turned, punched him in the gut until he doubled over, and then kneed him in the head, rendering him unconscious as well.

I stared at the three incapacitated bodies, still in a defensive stance in case one of them revived. When they didn't move for several seconds, I breathed a sigh of relief and relaxed.

Bruised, bloody, and breathless, I entered the Containment Room. It was completely bare and depressing, with no windows or decorations and only eleven beds lining the walls as furniture. It looked and felt like a prison.

At first, the children didn't know what to make of me. I actually felt out of place for not wearing the white pajama like outfits they had on.

"Hey, I'm Priss. I'm here to, uh, take you outta here," I said, breaking the awkward silence. They continued staring at me with these blank expressions. A young set of twins even hugged each other as if they were afraid of me.

Finally, a boy or man … well I don't really know what he was. I mean, he looked about my age in the face, but even through his clothes I could tell he had the body of a Greek God. Anyway, God Boy with piercing green eyes and thick dark hair gathered in a long ponytail approached me and said, "Do you know Madame Quindolyn?"

I was so distracted by his ridiculously cute French accent that at first I didn't know what to say. I didn't even recognize the name Madame Quindolyn. It sounded like the name of a circus psychic. Finally, I realized what he was talking about and stuttered, "She … she's my mother."

There was an audible collective sigh in the room.

"I am Specimen Mu," the boy said. "But I call myself Marco."

I had to withhold the urge to say, "Polo."

"May I?" he said, nodding toward my arm. I looked down and noticed the holes in my sweater and blood streaming out of them.

Holy hot dogs! I've been shot!

Marco took my arm gently and examined the damage.

"You've been shot twice in your right arm," he said.

"Good thing I'm left-handed," I said trying to lighten the mood.

He didn't get it or didn't appreciate the humor and just continued with his examination. "This one is a graze," he said pointing to my forearm. "But this one is a through and through." He sat me down on the bed. "We need to stop the bleeding." Marco kneeled in front of me, ripped up a bed sheet, and started cleaning my wounds with the pieces.

"I'll get the kids ready," a Russian accent said. I turned my head to the left and noticed a tall, pretty blond girl suddenly standing next to me.

"Whoa, when did she get there?" I asked as the girl walked away and started barking orders to the other specimens.

"That's Specimen Kappa. She has a tendency to blend into the background and just appear when you least expect it."

While he doctored my wounds, the room became a flurry of activity as the kids worked together, moving furniture to block doors and covering security cameras with bed sheets.

I just stared in awe. I had so many questions about these kids I didn't know where to start. Fortunately, he started explaining.

"I am fourteen. Kappa, or Katya as she prefers to be called, is fifteen. We are the oldest of the specimens who want to escape. There are twelve of us in all," Marco said while pressing a cloth to the bullet hole in my arm. "Specimens Xi and Omicron are younger, but they do not wish to escape. Xi even refused to accept a proper name."

"Trust me, I know Specimen Xi," I said, shaking off the memory of that crazy chick. "So is that why they keep you locked away? Because they're afraid you'll escape?" Marco nodded. "How long have you been forced to stay in the Containment Room with those things around your necks?"

"A few years ago, we started making psychic connections with your mother. A few of us have even been able to escape with her help. I was recaptured a few months ago and now they make us wear the inhibitors all the time as a precaution. Every day they force feed us propaganda and violence as they try to mold us into the killing machines they desire and counteract what your mother has shown us. She's shown us what a real life can be, and that's what we want now. All of us except Xi and Omicron."

"When did you escape?" Marco removed the now blood-soaked cloth he'd been pressing to my arm and applied another.

"Your mother helped me escape from here three years ago this December. I—"

"Wait a minute. Three years ago December? What date exactly?"

"December 17. Why?"

That was the date of my tenth birthday. That's why my mother wasn't at my birthday party. She was saving Marco's life. I guess some things are more important than a stupid game of Pin the Tail on the Donkey.

"No reason. Go on," I said.

"I remember I had just come back from a mission in Italy where I had to kill someone," he continued. "I still cannot get those images out of my mind." He closed his eyes and shook his head, smacking me in the face with his ponytail, but I didn't mind. His hair smelled like cinnamon and lilacs. "I decided I couldn't take it anymore. I didn't want to be a killer. Your mother came to get me. She moved me to France and then helped me get adopted. I was eleven years old. They were the only family I'd ever known." He looked sad. I wondered if his adoptive parents were dead or something, but I didn't want to get too personal. I'd only met this kid a few minutes ago, yet for some reason I felt so connected to him. I immediately wanted to know everything about him.

"What happened?" That seemed like a safe enough question. He could be as descriptive or evasive as he wanted to be. I imagined he was taken the same way I was a week ago, except he didn't have my awesome parents to come save him.

He sighed. "Once my adoptive parents found out about my ... abilities, they became afraid of me. I tried to explain what Colonel Selliwood had done to me and that it wasn't my fault, but they didn't want me anymore."

"Oh no."

"They actually contacted Colonel Selliwood. He came to get me, and now I'm here again. But because of you, soon I'll be free again. We'll all be free," he said, looking around the room.

"Speaking of being free, shouldn't we be on the move. I mean, they could be in here any second."

Marco looked at the wound again. "You've lost a lot of blood. You need to be in the best condition possible. If anything happens during the escape, you're the only one who will be able to defend us." He touched the collar on his neck. "Just a few more moments."

I sighed impatiently. I really wanted all of this to be over. But I decided to make the best of it and find out more. "You said you've formed telepathic connections with my mother. So you're a telepath, too?"

"We all are to some extent. Some more than others. We each just have to learn how to access that ability. You might have it as well since you are Madame Quindolyn's child."

"Me? No way. I've already started training and I haven't shown any signs of psychic ability. My brother, on the other hand, has had zero training and he can see the future." I don't know why I felt I could tell Marco this when I hadn't even told my mother. For some reason, I just felt I could trust him.

"Really? With no training? He must be incredibly powerful."

"Huh. You try telling *him* that."

"There, all done," he said, tying a piece of cloth around my arm.

"All right, let's go," I said, hopping up and waving everyone to the door. Katya picked up two small children and stepped behind me. Everyone else fell into line behind her.

In my impatience to get everyone out, I failed to consult the blueprint in my head. Everything was fine at first. We slithered along the walls super stealth style and avoided guards and sensors. But then I made a wrong turn into a room with no apparent exit. I turned to lead them out the way we came when suddenly the room flooded with armed guards. My chest tightened as I saw the disappointment in the children's eyes. I thought about fighting, but I counted thirty-seven guards. Even if the pajama-clad kids could help me, we were still way too out-numbered considering the glowing collars around their neck would prevent them from gaining any advantage.

"Josh, if you can hear me, I could really use your help right now." Whether Josh could hear me or not, I wasn't going out without a fight. They would have to take me outta here in a body bag. Unfortunately, according to Josh's vision, that's exactly what was going to happen.

Katya set down the children she'd been holding, and she and Marco took fighting stances on either side of me. They were willing to fight their way out too.

The guards aimed their guns and Ion Distorters, ready to fire at us. I thought this was the end when suddenly music started playing.

"What is that?" Marco asked.

"Um, it sounds like, Christina Aguilera."

"What is a Christina Aguilera?" Katya asked, cocking her head to the side like a confused puppy.

The guards dropped their weapons and started doing the choreography to Christina Aguilera's *Dirty*. They were shaking and twisting and striking poses that should be illegal for grown men to do.

"Thanks, Josh."

Tai must have been able to get the collar off, allowing Josh to try the mind control thing again with the guards. I wished he would have chosen a less gross song, though. I felt like I was getting a strip tease from the cast of *Rambo*.

We easily slipped past the dancing guards and into the corridor.

"I know the way from here," Marco said once we rounded a corner just past a weapons room. "If we go right, we'll be out in a few seconds."

I knew he was right, but I couldn't take my eyes off of what was to the left. The Central Control Room. In that moment, I knew what I had to do. "You lead everyone out. I'm going in."

I turned to leave, but Marco grabbed my hand, spun me around, and said, "Let me go with you."

"No way. No offense, but you won't be that much of a help with that thing around your neck." He touched his collar self-consciously and looked down at the ground. I could tell he wasn't used to being powerless. He probably felt pathetic not being able to help. "If you really want to help, get all of these kids outta here before I take this place down."

Marco lifted his head and nodded. I started to leave again, but he pulled me back. "I know you feel you have to do this, so I won't try to stop you," he said, staring into my eyes. "So, in case I never see you again ... I just want to say, thank you." He brought my hand to his lips and kissed it, sending a chill through me. I didn't know whether the chill came from the fact that a really cute boy that I'd just met was kissing me or from the fact that he too thought something bad was going to happen to me.

"Marco, it won't work," Katya called from behind him. Then she pointed to the inhibitor on her neck.

"I know. But I thought I'd try." He seemed sad as he turned away and ran toward where Katya and the others were headed.

What was that about? I tried not to dwell on it too much. I had a mission to accomplish.

I entered the Central Control Room and saw monitors, computers and blinking lights everywhere. Recalling the images my mother placed in my head when we were leaving the institute last week, my hands worked without my mind and I pressed the right sequence of buttons. A computer announced the beginning of a self-destruct sequence.

"There. That ought a do it." I turned to leave and almost fell over. Colonel Selliwood and another fighting machine blocked the only exit.

Chapter 29
Delta Dude

"What do you think you're doing?" Colonel Selliwood asked calmly.

"I'm stopping you from hurting any more children," I said with as much conviction as I could. I had to admit, I was pretty scared. And the way he was so freaking calm really freaked me out.

"You're stopping me?" he said, mocking my tone. "You think you can stop me? You think blowing up this place can stop me? You have no idea who you're dealing with."

As he spoke, I inched my way toward the exit. According to the computer, there were only five minutes until the entire place blew up. I wanted to get out of there as quickly as I could and hopefully without fighting Selliwood or the scary thing next to him.

Colonel Selliwood sat down at the computer terminal and pressed some buttons. He didn't even seem like he was in a hurry.

"I finally figured out the problem," he said, shaking his head. "The specimens think too much. Your mother has brainwashed you. She's brainwashed all of them. Good thing I've also figured out how to solve the problem. You're on the wrong side, little girl." He grabbed a couple of laptop computers and then said, "This has gone on long enough. Specimen Delta, finish her," before heading toward the door.

Delta looked at me and then back at Colonel Selliwood, his black waist-length dreadlocks swinging in the process. "Sir, she's a child," he said. "I think we should be able to place a collar on her like the other children." Wow, the robot-looking Delta dude sounded kinda human. Maybe he would spare me another fight.

Colonel Selliwood's head snapped around and he glared at Delta. "Just like I said. Too much thinking. Do what you're told. She must be destroyed."

"Yes, sir." So much for getting spared.

Delta walked toward me slowly, throwing knives that he pulled from every part of his body. I ducked and ran, hoping that eventually he'd run out of the tiny, sharp projectiles, but after forty seconds and about eighty knives, they were still coming. Then I realized that he was actually making the metal to form the two-inch pointed weapons. His body was apparently made of regenerative metal. That's why he looked so much like a robot.

Waiting him out was not an option, especially since there were less than three minutes left on the self-destruct sequence and portions of the institute were already starting to explode.

I did a series of flips toward him, trying to avoid the knives. I felt one slice into my thigh and another one went into my bullet hole wound that Marco had so diligently doctored. I wanted to cry out in pain, but I kept going. When in close range, I swept out his legs and then turned to smash his face in, but he'd already disappeared. He was as fast as Mom. I turned again and saw him standing behind me. Then he punched me so hard I landed across the room. I think I hit my head in the process because the room was spinning and it looked like there were five or six of him coming at me.

I didn't know what to do. I'd only had a few hours of training, I was bleeding in several places, and I was completely exhausted. There was no way I could beat him man-to-man, or man-to-girl as it was. It was time to pull out my secret weapon. It was time for a Prissy Fit.

I screamed at the top of my lungs, and then with tears streaming down my face, I yelled, "Oh my God, you hit me! I can't believe you hit me. I'm just a girl! How could you hit a little girl?"

Caught completely off-guard, Delta hesitated momentarily. Obviously, dealing with a crying girl had not been part of his training. I knew I didn't have a lot of time as I could already see his cold steely stare returning.

But his momentary lapse in judgment gave me just enough time to steady my aim and shoot. I blasted him with so much fire that he flew back against the wall. I kept bringing the fire until his partially metallic body began to melt and meld to the wall.

The computerized voice announced less than a minute until complete destruction. I turned and dashed for the door. I ran at top speed as burning parts of the building started falling around me. My clothing got charred, but the fire never even felt that hot against my skin. A weird feeling of déjà vu washed over me as I reached the outside and watched the institute erupt in flames … again. Didn't I just do this last week? Would I have to come back next week and do it again? When was it going to end?

I bent over, trying to cough the smoke and ash out of my lungs. Suddenly, I felt a pair of strong arms around my waist. Oh God, not more fighting. I didn't know how much more of this I could take. I grabbed the man's hand, twisted his arm around his back, and pinned him face down to the ground. With his other hand, he reached behind him, grabbed my neck, and flipped me over his head so that I landed on the ground on my back. He had to be inhuman to twist his arm to such an angle.

I hopped up and swung my leg around in a roundhouse kick. But before it could make contact with his head, he ducked and kicked my standing leg out from under me. I landed on top of him, our noses nearly touching.

"Marco?" I asked, staring into his green eyes.

"Sorry, I was just trying to hug you and then you attacked me and I guess my instincts kicked in."

Then there was a really weird moment where we just stared at each other. My heart raced. So did his.

I thought he was going to kiss me or something. Then I thought about Kyle. What the heck was I doing lying on top of this boy I'd just met? I quickly rolled off of Marco.

"Yeah, uh, sorry about that," I said, hopping to my feet.

I offered him my hand and helped him up. His white pajamas were covered in my blood. I looked over and saw the other Selliwood kids smiling and hugging each other. Their collars stopped glowing and I could actually see their powers returning. Two of the kids even started levitating. They could fly! Then one by one, they looked up into the sky. I followed their gazes and found what had captured their attention. It was a helicopter flying away from the ashes of the institute. Colonel Selliwood had escaped.

I could tell some of the kids wanted to go after him, but even though their powers had started to return, they weren't strong enough to catch that helicopter and fight the other specimens that were possibly on board. So we all just stood there and watched, knowing that one day we'd meet again.

Chapter 30

Tai, the Perfect Sidekick

"That was the coolest thing ever!" Chester said when the Selliwood kids and I reached the jet. He ran and jumped into my arms. Charlie was only a couple of steps behind him and also tackled me with a hug.

Those idiot boys didn't have the common sense to be terrified of the explosions that lit up the night sky. I knew their lack of fear would one day get them into loads of trouble. But, then again, I had to admit that what I'd just done was pretty cool. Unfortunately, the coolness of it quickly wore off as we stood around trying to figure out what to do next.

Mom and Dad were still unconscious. Josh held his head in his hands, too weak to walk or say more than three or four words at a time. I guessed the stunt with the guards took a lot of energy out of him.

"You okay, Josh?" I asked, rubbing his back.

He nodded. "Just … need … rest. Head … pain."

I kissed him on the cheek and then went to check on my best friend. Tai sat on the ground hugging her knees and staring blankly into the sky. She was frozen with fear. She really needed her Rock Box. I had to think of something to get her to snap out of it. I tried to hug her and tell her everything was gonna be all right, but she just kept staring into space.

"Tai, you're gonna make a horrible sidekick if you go all coma toast like this on me every time there's a little bit of danger."

Tai looked at me and said, "Do you mean comatose?"

"That's what I said. Coma toast."

She shook her head and then went back to staring at the sky.

Suddenly, I noticed all the Selliwood kids were looking at me, expecting me to give orders or say something smart or something.

"So, um, we should probably get out of here." They just kept staring at me. "Right, so, why don't we get in the jet?"

"You can fly the jet, Priss?" Charlie asked excitedly.

"That's awesome. You're the most awesome sister in the world, Priss," Chester added.

"Where are we gonna go, Priss? Where? Can we take the pajama kids home with us?" Charlie jumped up and down in front of me, probably looking forward to having twelve new people to torment at our house.

I opened my mouth to tell them where I would be taking the Selliwood kids when I realized I had no idea. I couldn't very well bring them to River's Bend and claim they were my cousins or something. They were too quiet, well-behaved, and obedient. No one would ever believe they were related to a Sumner.

"May I make a suggestion?" Marco asked, noticing my confusion. I nodded. I was up for any ideas. "Your mother created a safe house where she takes all the escapees before transporting them to a permanent home. Specimen W is the caretaker."

"Perfect. We'll go there."

"The only problem is, I am not sure of the location. She never told me, in case I was tortured into giving it away."

"Great," I threw my arms in the air theatrically. "I'll just go get a phone book and look up Secret Selliwood Survivor Safe House. I'm sure we'll find an address in no time."

Then I heard Tai's shaky voice say, "If Mrs. Sumner flew there, the coordinates should be in the jet's navigational memory."

"Do you think you could take a look at the computer system and try to find it?" I asked.

"Yeah, I think I can," she said, a spark starting to return to her eye.

Tai sat in the pilot's seat and started poking around the jet's computer. Moments later, everything started shaking.

"I didn't know Colorado had earthquakes," I said.

"Neither did I."

Tai and I gave each other a panicked look. A large rock hit the windshield of the jet. Tai screamed. I jumped up and ran outside as Tai's fingers went back to working the computer.

Pieces of the mountain were crumbling. A huge boulder dislodged and started rolling to where my little brothers were thumb wrestling each other, completely oblivious to the danger around them. I ran to grab them, but Marco beat me to it.

"What's going on?" I asked as he brought the boys to me.

"The explosions from the institute must have rocked the foundation of the mountain. I think it's coming down."

I looked at the ground and saw a crack develop between my feet. We didn't have much time.

"Everyone on the jet, now!" I yelled. I looked around, making sure everyone was getting on board. "Josh!" I yelled noticing he was still on the ground, clutching his head.

"I'll get him," Katya said, coming out of nowhere and sweeping Josh up into her arms. Wow. She was strong. She carried him like a baby into the jet, the whole time not taking her eyes off his face. *Huh* ...

After everyone was in their seats, I dashed to the cockpit.

"Find anything?" I asked Tai as I picked her up and placed her in the copilot seat. I didn't wait for her response as I initiated the take-off sequence.

Tai buckled her safety belt. "Yeah, the coordinates that are logged in the most, besides the woods near River's Bend, are found in Kansas. I think that's where it must be. I already programmed them into the navigational system."

"Good work, Tai."

She took a deep breath and smiled. *Maybe she will be the perfect sidekick after all.*

Chapter 31

The Good-bye Girl

Josh recovered from the draining use of his powers in a matter of hours. Dad woke up next. Though he still had the broken leg I'd given him earlier, plus several new broken bones in his face, hands, and ribs, he was still better off than Mom. She kept going in and out of consciousness, mumbling things like, "Don't touch my children," and "Kill me if you have to."

Thankfully, since the entire town was at the River Day Dance the night of the phony arrest, we didn't have to explain the whole "taken at gunpoint" thing to anyone. The only person who saw anything was our neighbor, Mr. Grayson, and his credibility was shot since he often got too drunk to find a bathroom and used the nearest lamppost as a substitute. A few people did wonder about the helicopter in the sky that night, but Tai took care of that. She took the holographic game of *Tetris* from the jet, made a few adjustments, and then went on *Channel 2 News* with Stacy Marguilles again. She convinced everyone that the helicopter was part of her science fair project in holographic technology. She was even able to recreate the helicopter, complete with sound effects. Like I said, perfect sidekick.

"Once again, Taiana, you amaze me. You are sure to win the science fair this year," Stacy Marguilles said after Tai's demonstration. "And now back to Tom with a report on Colorado's most powerful earthquake in over one hundred years."

I thought having everything logically explained to the people of River's Bend would be enough. I thought we'd be able to slip back into our normal routine and pretend the Selliwood Institute had never existed. Deep down I knew that wasn't going to happen. Dr. Witherall and Colonel Selliwood knew where we lived. They'd already found us twice. They were both still alive and well, and at any moment, they could come after us again. After being back for only two days, Dad decided it'd be best if we left Pennsylvania.

"You know, you really should be coming with us," I told Tai as she helped me pack the last few things in my room. Once Dad decided we were moving, Josh and I stayed home from school and worked on packing up the house round the clock. By Wednesday afternoon, we were ready to go. "They know who you are. What if they come after you?"

Tai shook her head. "What could they possibly want with *me*? Besides, I can't leave my parents. They're the only family I've ever known. They're all I have."

"I can be your family. We *are* family. You're the closest thing I have to a sister."

Tai dropped the blanket she was folding and crossed the room to hug me. We both broke into tears.

"I made you something," she said after a few minutes of crying. She wiped the tears from her eyes and then went to grab her purse off of the window seat. "Here you go," she said, handing me a huge metal hairbrush that she'd pulled out of her purse. "I didn't have time to wrap it. It took me hours to get it working properly."

I took the metal monstrosity into my hands, turning it over and over. Why in the world would she make me a hairbrush? A butt-ugly hairbrush at that.

"Um, thanks?"

"I know it's not much to look at, but it's completely functional."

Wow, a *functional* hairbrush as a going away present from my best friend of four years. This was possibly the worst gift ever, but I didn't want to hurt her feelings so I put it to my head and tried to use it.

"Ow!" Not only was it totally ugly, but it was ridiculously painful.

"What are you doing?" Tai asked, staring at me like I was some sort of moron.

"I'm trying to use your gift."

"Well, that's not how you use it."

I stared at the brush again. What was I missing?

"Priss, it's not really a hairbrush. Do you really think I'd give you an ugly hairbrush as a gift? Please. What kind of friend do you take me for?" She snatched the brush out of my hands and pushed a button on the end of it. Immediately, her purse started ringing. "See! It's a communication device. A little rudimentary, but it was all I could do in such little time." She opened her purse and pulled out a black compact. "You can only call this compact, but at least we can keep in touch. The range is a little over two thousand miles, so hopefully you won't move farther away than that. I made it in the shape of a brush because I knew your dad would never let you have a real cell phone, but how could he possibly object to you having a hairbrush? Every girl needs a hairbrush. What do you think?"

"Wow, Tai, this is like beyond genius," I said, looking at the brush phone in a new light.

"I'm glad you like it." Tai smiled, completely pleased with herself.

We got so involved in playing with the brush phone and planning times to talk to each other that neither one of us noticed when the doorbell rang.

"Someone's at the door for you," Chester said, bursting into my room unannounced.

"Yeah, someone's at the door," Charlie repeated, adding kissing noises, which could only mean it was Kyle. Once things calmed down a little after the Selliwood situation, I had to explain that I'd snuck out of the house to meet Kyle the night everyone was captured. So, in Charlie and Chester's little minds, he was my boyfriend. Unfortunately, that wasn't exactly true. Since I hadn't been in school all week, I hadn't spoken to him since the night I ditched him at the gazebo. He probably hated me.

"So, it's true? You're really moving away?" Kyle said, turning around and around my empty living room. "There was a rumor at school, but I didn't think you'd really leave without saying good-bye to me." He looked really hurt. I didn't know what to say.

"I'm sorry, Kyle. My dad just decided a couple of days ago and—"

"Is it because of me? You hate me, don't you? Is it because I told everyone in school I was going to kiss you before I told you? That was dumb. I know. I'm sorry. I probably freaked you out. Is that why you ditched me at the gazebo?"

"No, Kyle, this has nothing to do with you."

"Please don't move, Priss. You're my best friend. Who else am I gonna ride bikes with or share my comic book collection with? And you're the only girl I've ever wanted to kiss."

I felt more tears coming. I didn't want to cry in front of Kyle, though. So, instead, I wrapped my arms around him and buried my face in his chest. This was gonna be harder than I expected. I'd already had the three-hour screaming match with my father telling him how unfair it was we were moving. But he told me to just accept it. It was for the best. How would I feel if next time Kyle was kidnapped instead of Tai and I wasn't able to save him? It's pretty depressing to know that your simple existence put everyone you loved in danger.

Even though I'd spent two days mentally preparing myself for leaving Kyle, right now, wrapped in his arms, I didn't know if I could do it. I'd spent the weekend defeating genetically enhanced assassins and maniacal villains, yet I wasn't strong enough to let go of a crush. I was pathetic.

Seconds later, Josh entered the living room carrying a large box. "Priss, Dad says we're getting on the road in ten minutes," he said before going outside to put the box in the U-Haul trailer. Tai was right behind him, loading the last box from my room. Kyle and I were still locked in a bear hug. Neither one of us wanted to let go first.

Finally, I said, "I gotta go, Kyle," and pushed away. Hand in hand, we walked out of the front door, onto my porch. Charlie and Chester were already buckled into their booster seats in the Escalade. Mom was asleep in the front passenger seat. The plan was Dad would drive the Escalade with a U-Haul trailer attached, Josh would drive his truck with another U-Haul attached to it, and I would follow from above in the jet.

"Do you at least know your new address so we can keep in touch?"

"I don't even know what state we're moving to." Dad wouldn't tell me for fear that in a moment of weakness, I'd tell Kyle or Tai. He'd flip if he knew about the brush phone.

"Well, I guess this is it then. I might never see you again."

"Don't worry, Kyle. I have a feeling River's Bend hasn't seen the last of me. I'll be back."

Chapter 32

Super Mom

My mom no longer had her powers. That's what the machine she was attached to at Selliwood had done to her. It was an experimental procedure that stripped the genetic mutations off of her DNA, causing excruciating amounts of pain. Apparently, my mother was the guinea pig for the procedure. I wonder if they had planned to use it on the kids later.

My mother hoped her body would revert to its natural state, thus returning her powers, but until then, she was adjusting to life as a *normal* person. Josh and Dad took care of the farm we lived on in Missouri that happened to be only about thirty minutes away from the safe house in Kansas. Farmer Dad was pretty comical. He took the farming thing so seriously. Did he really need a 9 mm to blow a hole in the earth before dropping in a watermelon seed? Probably not. But what else was he going to do with his gun collection.

Anyway, while Josh and Dad turned into farmers, Mom turned into super housewife. Every day we woke up to homemade biscuits and gravy or pancakes and sausage. She turned the living room into a classroom and became our daily teacher since Dad wouldn't let us go to public school. She even invited the Selliwood kids over once a week and cooked a big family dinner.

It seemed like Mom really enjoyed her new role as full-time mother and wife. And while it was nice to have her around all the time, I had to admit, I kinda missed the superhero.

My thirteenth birthday caught me by surprise. I mean, once you discover you can shoot fire out of your fingers, fly a jet, and save your family from evil villains, being able to get into PG-13 movies sort of loses its luster. Thankfully, Mom was paying more attention to things than I was. She planned a big bash for me, invited some of the Selliwood kids, and quarantined Charlie and Chester so they wouldn't ruin things and embarrass me. Even though it was the middle of December, I got to have a pool party. Given my abilities, the pool turned into more of a hot tub.

The party was a huge success. Though snow surrounded us, we were all perfectly toasty in the steaming hot pool. I even started a bonfire where we roasted marshmallows and made s'mores. Then we played a game that I named Super Cannon Ball Tag. It was a cross between Freeze Tag and Cannon Ball. Basically, we ran around tagging each other, and if you got caught, Pi or Rho would fly to you, pick you up, and drop you into the pool like a cannon ball.

It was so stupid yet so fun at the same time. That was until Marco got caught. Pi, whose chosen name was Peter, picked him up and dropped him in the pool. No problem, right? Wrong. When Marco climbed out of the water, his wet t-shirt clung to every delicious muscle of his chest. And then it got worse. He whipped his shirt off and shook his long glorious hair. I swear it happened in slow motion.

And then something really strange happened. I started crying. Not a few stray tears; I'm talking shoulder-sagging, stomach-clutching, boo-hoo sobbing. I ran to my room and shut the door. After flopping on the bed, I continued with the mysterious crying. Why was it that the sight of Marco reduced me to tears? And then it hit me. When I first left River's Bend, I thought about Kyle constantly. I cried every night because I missed him so much. But in the last few days, I hadn't thought about him at all. And then I found myself attracted, I mean really attracted, to Marco. What did that say about me?

Why couldn't things just be the way they were? I missed Kyle. I missed Tai even though I secretly spoke to her every night on the brush phone. I missed the annual Winter Ice Festival in River's Bend. I even missed losing to the eighth grade in the obligatory snowball fight after the first snow of the season.

"You okay in there, Prissy?" my mom asked through the door. The old me would have told her to go away, but in the past few months, my mom and I had gotten really close. Now the thought of talking to her about my problems didn't repulse me. I kinda looked forward to spending time with her.

"No, I'm not okay. Nothing's okay. I hate my life."

My mom came into my room and wrapped a towel around me as she sat next to me on the bed.

"I know you're in a lot of pain and you miss your friends and your life in River's Bend," she said, rubbing my back.

Suddenly, I felt very selfish. Sure there were a ton of things I missed, but I didn't even consider how my mother might be feeling. Her entire existence was different.

"Mom, do you miss your powers?"

"Not as much as I've missed *you* over the past four years."

I started crying even harder as I hugged her tight. "I love you, Mom."

"I love you, too," she said. "And I hate to see you so upset. How about I make you a deal?"

"What kind of deal?" I asked, wiping my tears and looking at her. She looked a different kind of beautiful. Instead of a white cat suit with a superhero utility belt, she wore a white apron and a belt that held a spatula and a soup ladle.

"How about I let you see Kyle and Tai again. Not just once, but on a regular basis. Maybe every other weekend or something."

"What's the catch?"

"Well, I don't mind that Tai knows everything. I completely trust her. After what she went through with us, I consider her an honorary Sumner. But Kyle is a problem. We just can't afford to let someone else know about us."

"So what do you suggest?"

"You've met Kappa, haven't you? Or Katya as she prefers to be called." I nodded. "Well, do you know what her ability is?" I shook my head. "She can erase short-term memory."

"Are you suggesting that we erase Kyle's memory after every time I see him?"

"Not his entire memory. Just the part that reveals our location."

I thought about this for a second. I really wanted to see Kyle, but erasing his memory all the time just didn't sound safe. What if we caused permanent brain damage?

"I don't know, Mom. Will it hurt him?"

"I assure you, it's perfectly safe. Katya and I have been practicing."

I started thinking of the possibilities. I might be able to have a normal relationship with Kyle. Well, normal for me. That'll have to do.

"Okay, let's do it," I said, so excited I thought I'd burst. I couldn't wait to plan their first visit. Oh, a trip to the mall was definitely in order. I needed a new dress if I was going to see Kyle for the first time in two months.

"I thought you'd say that," she said with a grin. "So, Katya and I flew to River's Bend this morning and picked up your present. Come on in, guys," my mother called into the hallway. Then in walked my two best friends.

"Surprise!" Kyle and Tai yelled in unison.

I jumped off the bed and screamed while tackling them both with a hug. We jumped around my room crying and laughing and hugging. I think I even saw a few tears from Kyle.

I spent the next couple of hours showing Kyle and Tai around my new home. I even introduced them to the Selliwood kids, who tried their best to be normal for Kyle's sake.

"I am Marco. It is nice to meet some of Priscilla's friends. She has told me a lot about you," he said, shaking hands with Kyle.

"That's a cool accent. Where is it from?" Kyle asked.

"France. I speak French as well as sixteen other languages."

I stared at Marco. Why had he never told me that? I'd known him for over two months and we'd spent a lot of time together. Granted, I always did most of the talking. "Seventeen languages? I didn't know that. I can't even name seventeen languages!" I said a little too enthusiastically.

Kyle's demeanor changed. He put on his angry face, the face he wears whenever he's about to lose at something. He looked back and forth between Marco and me a couple of times before saying, "I can. I can name seventeen languages. English, Spanish, French, German … Canadian—"

"Canadians speak English or French. Either way, it doesn't count. You're still at four," Marco said, crossing his arms.

Uh oh. This isn't good.

Kyle glared at him. "Fine. Italian, Russian, Portuguese … Brazilian."

"Nope. Sorry. Brazilian is not a language. They speak Portuguese in Brazil."

"I knew that," Kyle said, taking a step toward Marco. That's when I noticed Marco's fingers turning into metal and curving into a fist. Definitely, not good.

"I'll give you seven. Only ten more to go. Or can you count that high?"

I wasn't sure why Marco was being so crabby, but I knew it was time for me to end this before someone got hurt, namely Kyle.

"Uh, Tai, come here," I called to Tai who was talking to Josh on the other side of the room. "Tai, Marco. Marco, Tai," I introduced them as if they'd never met before. "Tai is going to Copenhagen soon, so she's learning Danish. Why don't you two go off and talk about … languages or something," I said, pleading with Tai with my eyes. She picked up on my cue and led Marco toward the pool. Then I grabbed Kyle and led him out of the house.

"I don't like that guy, Priss. Is he at your house a lot?" Kyle said when we started walking along the wooden gate around our farm.

"No, not that often," I lied. Truth was Marco had been coming over a lot. Even more often than the weekly "family" dinners. But I wasn't about to tell Kyle that.

We fell into a warm, cozy silence as Kyle finally started to calm down. After a few minutes, he grabbed my hand and we kept walking toward the sunset.

Finally he said, "I like you, Priss. I really, really like you. I've liked you since the third grade, unfortunate hair and all." He tugged his big North Face jacket closed with his free hand to fight off the cold. *I wonder if he'd notice if I warmed his hand up a little. On second thought, I'd better not risk it.*

"I like you, too, Kyle."

"Nothing's been the same since you left. I know there's some big important reason why you had to move away, but I really miss you and I still really want to be a part of your life."

"I miss you, too, Kyle." What the heck was wrong with me? Why couldn't I think of anything more original to say? I guess I just couldn't get my mind off the fact that this might be it. My first kiss might happen any second. The more I thought about kissing him, though, the guiltier I felt. It would be unfair to him. If he knew the truth about me and my family, he'd probably run away screaming and not look back. It would be best if we were just friends.

"Well, I've been thinking," he added, just as snowflakes began to fall. It was beyond romantic. "Just because we don't live in the same town anymore doesn't mean we can't be together. Why don't we try a long-distance relationship? We can make it work." He stopped walking and stood in front of me, melting my resolve with his fiery blue eyes. I'd forgotten how completely gorgeous he was. I had to turn away. Staring at the ground, I sighed. Poor Kyle. He had no idea what he was asking. I could never be a normal girlfriend.

Shaking my head, I said, "Kyle, I don't think—" Before I could finish my thought, he grabbed me by the waist, pulled me close, and placed his lips on mine. A thousand butterflies cart wheeled in my stomach. I seriously think I saw stars.

That kiss changed everything. Being in his arms felt too good to pass up. There was no way I could let him go.

So what if we couldn't have a *normal* relationship. What was normal, anyway? Who got to decide that? So what if my closest friends could read minds, turn into metal, or fly? So what if I'd have to erase my boyfriend's memory every once in a while? So what if, to my parents, grounding meant taking away the keys to an invisible jet? I loved them all, and they loved me. That was as normal as I needed to be.

Chapter 33

The Shooter

My mind wouldn't turn off. Having super hearing is really annoying sometimes. I mean, I could hear Charlie and Chester arguing over who was the bigger boogerhead even though their room was on the other side of the house. I felt like running over there and reminding them that they were identical twins. If one of them was a boogerhead, so was the other. Idiots.

I sighed. Even if I could fall asleep, I wasn't sure if I really wanted to. Selliwood happened almost three months ago, I'd just had an awesome pool party and gotten my first kiss, and yet I still had nightmares. Amazingly, the only thing that helped was Josh. He was able to calm me the same way Mom used to.

"Can't sleep?" Josh asked as soon as I poked my head into his room. I didn't even have to say anything. He knew I was there. He was getting really good at the psychic thing.

I pushed open the door and stepped through. "I hate my photographic memory. I can't get the images out of my head."

"Try being psychic," he said, swinging his feet over the side of his bed. Then he sent me that calm feeling. I finally felt relaxed. "I can't sleep either. How about I beat you in a couple of games of *Street Mania* to get our minds off of things?"

"You're on." I sat down in front of Josh's TV and clicked it on while he pulled out the controllers from under his bed.

Josh was even easier to beat than usual. Normally, he can hang with me for at least halfway through a course. That night I was basically blowing him away right after the starting gun. I could tell something was on his mind.

"I'm having the vision again," he said after I'd beaten him seven or eight times.

"What vision?"

"Your death."

I hadn't thought about his vision of my death in three months. When it didn't come true at Selliwood, I just figured he'd made a mistake.

I paused the game. "Tell me about it. What did you see?"

He closed his eyes. "You were shot in the chest at point-blank range."

"So, it's the same as before? It didn't come true, Josh. You were wrong."

Josh shook his head, eyes still closed. "No. It's not the same. One thing is different. This time I can see who shoots you."

"Who is it? Is it Xi? I knew she'd come back for revenge." I stood up and pounded my fist into my hand. *If it's a fight she wants, she can have it.*

"No, it's not Xi."

"Then who? Tell me. Who's the shooter?"

"It's Tai."